THE FORTUNES OF TEXAS

Follow the lives and loves of a complex family with a rich history and deep ties in the Lone Star State

DIGGING FOR SECRETS

A ruse brings six estranged Fortunes to Chatelaine, Texas, to supposedly have their most secret wishes granted. They're thrilled—until they discover someone is seeking vengeance for a long-ago wrong...and turning their lives upside down!

Fortune's Lone Star Twins

West Fortune was convinced he'd make a terrible father, so Tabitha Buckingham ended their engagement, not realizing he'd soon have to fake his own death to protect her—or that she was pregant with his twins! Now, he wants to be the dad he never had...but is he willing to be a family man all the way?

T0021471

Dear Reader,

Welcome back to Chatelaine, Texas, and the world of the legendary Fortune family!

This is my first book for the long-running Fortunes of Texas series, and I could not be more thrilled to be part of this amazing collection of books. This latest Fortunes of Texas miniseries is called Digging for Secrets, and *Fortune's Lone Star Twins* is the fourth book. Make sure to pick up the first three books in this miniseries to get the full effect of everything going on with the Fortune family in Chatelaine, Texas. You can find them at Harlequin.com or any online retailer.

Did you know that the Fortunes of Texas has been an ongoing series for more than twenty years and has included some of Harlequin's most beloved authors? I was so honored to write this book, and not just because I've lived in the great state of Texas for my entire life, y'all.

Fortune's Lone Star Twins tells the story of Tabitha Buckingham and West Fortune. In the opening chapter, Tabitha gets the shock of her life when her long-lost fiancé comes back from the dead. But soon, West is the one who's the most surprised when he discovers he's the daddy to one-year-old twins. And that's only the start! This story and the entire miniseries are full of dramatic twists and turns.

Look for more from the Fortunes in the rest of The Fortunes of Texas: Digging for Secrets miniseries, coming soon!

Happy reading,

Teri

FORTUNE'S LONE STAR TWINS

Teri Wilson

Special thanks and acknowledgment are given to Teri Wilson for her contribution to The Fortunes of Texas: Digging for Secrets miniseries.

ISBN-13: 978-1-335-59483-9

Fortune's Lone Star Twins

Copyright © 2024 by Harlequin Enterprises ULC

Recycling programs for this product may not exist in your area.

For questions and comments about the quality of this book, please contact us at CustomerService@Harlequin.com.

® is a trademark of Harlequin Enterprises ULC.

Harlequin Enterprises ULC
22 Adelaide St. West, 41st Floor
Toronto, Ontario M5H 4E3, Canada
www.Harlequin.com

Printed in Lithuania

MIX
Paper | Supporting responsible forestry
FSC® C021394

USA TODAY bestselling author **Teri Wilson** writes heartwarming romance for Harlequin Special Edition. Three of Teri's books have been adapted into Hallmark Channel Original Movies, most notably *Unleashing Mr. Darcy*. She is also a recipient of the prestigious RITA® Award for excellence in romantic fiction and a recent inductee into the San Antonio Women's Hall of Fame.

Teri has a special fondness for cute dogs and pretty dresses, and she loves following the British royal family. Visit her at www.teriwilson.net.

Books by Teri Wilson

The Fortunes of Texas: Digging for Secrets

Fortune's Lone Star Twins

Harlequin Special Edition

Love, Unveiled

Her Man of Honor
Faking a Fairy Tale

Lovestruck, Vermont

Baby Lessons
Firehouse Christmas Baby
The Trouble with Picket Fences

Furever Yours

How to Rescue a Family
A Double Dose of Happiness

Drake Diamonds

His Ballerina Bride
The Princess Problem
It Started with a Diamond

Visit the Author Profile page
at Harlequin.com for more titles.

In loving memory of my sister-in-law, Ramona Bonnet.

We miss you so much, Mona. xoxo

Chapter One

"Bless your heart, Tabitha. Do you have any plans for Mother's Day later this month?"

Tabitha Buckingham bristled as Courtney Riddle blinked her tacky eyelash extensions in her general direction. The other four moms in her weekly moms-of-multiples playgroup immediately followed suit, blessing Tabitha's pathetic little heart in silent unison.

For the record, her heart wasn't pathetic, and it most definitely didn't need to be blessed. Here in Texas, that saying was more often a passive-aggressive insult than an expression of genuine concern. Tabitha had lived in the Lone Star State her entire life. She knew Texas girl snark when she heard it.

Or maybe Tabitha was simply so well acquainted with this specific form of regional vernacular because her heart had been blessed on a daily basis for the past nineteen months straight.

The *other* playgroup moms meant well. All of the members of the group had met during their pregnancies at a special Lamaze class for moms of multiples. After navigating the ups and downs of their unique pregnancies together, they'd decided to keep the group intact and start visiting once a week for baby playdates. While the moms sat cross-legged in a big circle, the babies and toddlers crawled, pulled up and played with a variety of brightly colored toys in the center of Courtney's expansive playroom. Tabitha didn't know what she would've done without the other moms—with the obvious exception of today's host, who never missed a chance to remind Tabitha that she was the only single mother in their ranks.

What, exactly, was Courtney's point? It wasn't as if Tabitha could forget.

Hmm, I haven't seen the father of my children in a while. I wonder where he is...

Oh, that's right. He died before I could even tell him I was pregnant. Silly me, his brutal murder must have slipped my mind.

She could chalk a lot of mental fog up to baby brain, particularly in the early months just after the twins had been born, but Tabitha had never once forgotten what had become of West Fortune. Bless her heart, sometimes she really wished she could.

"It's okay, hon. We know that West would do something sweet for you for Mother's Day if he was still here." Patsy Mercer, one of Tabitha's best friends in the playgroup, reached over and gave her hand a squeeze. "God rest his soul."

Tabitha's throat went thick at the mention of West's name. She didn't care a whit about being pampered on Mother's Day, though. Courtney had just waxed poetic for five full minutes about how she expected her husband to make her breakfast in bed for the special day.

"Real, homemade waffles, *not* the frozen kind," she'd been sure to specify with a loaded glance at Tabitha.

On the one-year anniversary of West's death, Tabitha had broken down crying in the frozen food aisle of GreatStore, the big box store that was the only place in town to buy groceries. Time had been such a blur of round-the-clock feedings and diaper changes that she'd regularly lost track of what day of the week it was, much less the exact calendar date. But then she'd glanced at the expiration date on a box of frozen waffles and somehow, she'd known. Her *soul* had known, even though she'd done her level best not to dwell on West's passing. She had twin infants to raise, a home to take care of and a small web design business to run—all by herself. Her former fiancé was gone, and nothing was going to bring him back.

Of course Courtney had stumbled upon Tabitha's rare moment of weakness in the grocery store and taken the opportunity to remind her that organic, homemade waffles were far healthier for growing babies than processed, frozen alternatives. Tabitha had simply blinked away her tears and pretended to listen while her mind spun with memories of West's gruff laugh, his deep Texas drawl and the way her heart always turned over in her chest when he glanced up at her from beneath the brim of his black Stetson. Tabitha had always teased him about his black hat. He'd been an attorney—a county prosecutor. Quite literally, one of the good guys.

Black Stetson notwithstanding.

Tabitha had refused to keep listening to Courtney's

lecture about *proper nutrition* for children while memories of West tugged at her heartstrings. In the end, she'd tossed the box of waffles into her shopping basket with a tad too much force and pushed her cart straight past Courtney, accidentally rolling over the pointy toe of the other mom's designer shoe in the process. That little mortifying incident had taken place more than six months ago, but the pesky woman obviously wasn't ready to let it go.

"It's fine," Tabitha said around the lump in her throat. "*We're* fine. The twins and I have plans with my sisters for Mother's Day."

Liar, liar, pants on fire.

Tabitha had no such plans with Lily and Haley... yet. She and her triplet sisters had been separated as infants after their parents were killed in a car accident, but they'd reconnected now as adults. Lily and Haley had even been Tabitha's birthing coaches. She made a mental note to call them and set something up.

"What are you doing for Mother's Day, Patsy?" Tabitha cast a beseeching glance at her friend in an effort to steer the conversation away from West's gaping absence.

Mother's Day, she could handle. Thinking about West and how different everything would be if he hadn't been shot and killed by a vengeful ex-con he'd helped put in prison? Not so much.

Patsy brightened. "We're having a Mother's Day brunch with my parents after church on Sunday. Last year Gabe gave Mom and me matching orchid corsages to wear for the day."

The mom sitting on Patsy's other side pressed a hand to her heart. "I just love that sweet Southern tradition."

Tabitha nodded and awwwed along with the rest of the group, even though she'd completely forgotten that Mother's Day corsages were a thing. Something told her she wouldn't be getting a flower to pin to her dress this year.

"You know what? This morning has been crazy. The boys didn't get their regular nap before we came today." Tabitha stood. She needed to get out of here. This nagging sense of wistfulness was getting to be too much. Because, truth be told, she had no reason whatsoever to expect that things would've been different even if West were still alive. "I should get Zach and Zane and put them down for a bit before it gets too close to dinnertime."

"Are you sure? The boys seem fine," Patsy said, casting a glance toward the center of the room where the twins were pounding the colorful keys of a musical activity table with their pudgy little hands. One of Courtney's little girls toddled between them, playing along nicely with Zane and Zach. Thankfully, Courtney's twins hadn't seemed to inherit the mean girl gene. Not yet, anyway.

"You know how it is. Kids can be fine one minute and cranky the next," Tabitha said as she maneuvered the boys into their double stroller. Zane grinned up at her, and for a second, his eyes looked so much like his daddy's that Tabitha's smile went wobbly. She swallowed. Hard. "Sorry to cut things short this time."

Courtney stood to walk Tabitha to the door. Play-group never met at Tabitha's house because her tiny two-bedroom home in Chatelaine's town center was already a tight squeeze with two babies—never mind ten more.

"Don't you worry a bit about having to go. I just can't imagine how difficult things must be for you, doing it all on your own." Courtney batted her ridiculous eyelashes, and Tabitha's teeth ground together.

Don't say it. Please don't... I'm begging you.

"Bless your heart."

Tabitha made three full loops around Chatelaine in her small SUV before heading to her house near the center of town. Full disclosure: she hadn't exactly been truthful about the twins missing their morning nap time. The boys had slept like little angels while she'd gotten caught up on a website design project for a new client based in San Antonio.

But after the onslaught of feelings at playgroup, she could use a little quiet time before she jumped back into her workday. Tabitha doubted she'd get much accomplished today, anyway. The high school student who usually helped her out with the twins in the afternoons had recently given her notice because she'd made the cheerleading squad. Tabitha was thrilled for her, of course. In small-town Texas, football and cheerleading were Very Big Deals. Unfortunately, juggling two babies while also working at home wasn't exactly small potatoes either.

Like most babies, Zach and Zane loved the soothing

motion of a moving automobile, so taking the scenic route home seemed like a mighty fine idea. Not that there was much to see in Chatelaine, which by Texas-sized standards, was truly a one-horse town. Aside from GreatStore and the Chatelaine Museum, the only highlights were the collection of grand, arched gates that led to tree-lined paths and sprawling ranches just outside of town. And the mines, of course.

For a while, Chatelaine had attracted prospectors and fortune hunters, convinced the town held an underground treasure trove of gold, silver and copper. That had been years ago—way before Tabitha's time. The mining operations came to an abrupt end after a terrible tragedy in 1965 when one of the mines collapsed, but tourists and hikers still came to town to explore the abandoned mines. Some of the properties featured guided tours and gift shops. Tabitha's stomach rumbled as she passed a hand-painted sign advertising homemade fudge at one such establishment.

Nope. She made an abrupt U-turn and guided the car back toward home. *Not going there—not today of all days.*

The last gift West had given her had been a batch of fudge from that very shop. "Sweets, because I'm sweet on you," he'd said as he'd handed her the white box, tied with a pink satin ribbon. When she'd opened it, she'd found an engagement ring nestled inside, sparkling like mad among the chocolate. Tabitha still wore the ring on a chain around her neck, tucked beneath her clothes so no one could see. Her little secret.

Which *definitely* needed to stop. She had no right

to wear that diamond solitaire anymore, but after West died, she simply couldn't bring herself to stop. Even if sometimes it made her feel like the biggest fraud in the world.

"We were broken up," she whispered.

Tabitha had only uttered those words out loud a handful of times. For months after West's murder, she hadn't told a soul. Why would she? West was the love of her life. Breaking off their engagement had been the hardest choice Tabitha had ever made, and when she'd finally done it—once she'd finally managed to tell him that they couldn't have a future if he didn't want children—it had all been for nothing. West had been shot and killed the very next morning before anyone found out they were no longer getting married. And irony of ironies, completely unbeknownst to her, Tabitha had already been pregnant with West's babies.

Once she found out she was pregnant, she'd confided in her sisters about the breakup. Recently, she'd also shared the truth with Bea Fortune, West's cousin. Bea had been over visiting the twins and blurted out that she'd recently discovered she was pregnant. Entrusted with Bea's news, Tabitha had shared her secret truth, as well. But they were the only three people who knew.

Tabitha's memories of the night before West's murder felt so surreal now, almost like a fever dream, and she couldn't force herself to face them. When snippets of their breakup came back to her during the funeral, she'd nearly vomited in the church pew. Later that afternoon, after she'd watched the two little lines appear on an at-home pregnancy test, she'd taken her engagement ring out of her nightstand drawer and slid it onto the delicate chain West had given her the previous Christmas. Both the necklace and the ring were crafted from gold from a mine owned by the Fortune family out in West Texas—not the Chatelaine mine, but another one that held hidden treasures deep underground. In the beginning, Tabitha had loved wearing something with such a meaningful family connection. But now, after the split and West's shocking death, it seemed like a bad omen—as if her engagement ring had been cursed by the same twist of fate that had brought down the mine in Chatelaine all those years ago.

"We were broken up," she said again, louder this time. Maybe if she repeated it enough times, she'd finally internalize the truth and those fleeting, what-could-have-been fantasies would stop invading her thoughts in her most vulnerable moments.

One of the twins stirred at the sound of her voice, and Tabitha stole a glance at the rearview mirror. Zach's tiny rosebud mouth puckered and he let out a whimper.

"It's okay," she soothed. "Don't cry, sweetie. Everything's okay. We're all okay."

Because they *were* okay. She and her babies were just fine on their own. Tabitha had experienced another silly moment of weakness, that's all.

Still, she tugged the chain from beneath the collar of her blouse and wrapped her fingers around her engagement ring, squeezing it tight. The metal was warm from resting in the secret place against her heart.

She held it for a beat, savoring her good memories of West—clinging to them while once again pushing their breakup to the back of her mind, one last time.

Zach settled back into a quiet sleep as the car crawled through tiny downtown Chatelaine, and Tabitha let out a sigh as she turned onto her street. She was happy to be home—away from the wistfulness that had come over her at playgroup and back to her normal life with her boys. All she'd ever wanted was to be a mom. She knew she was lucky to have been adopted after her parents' accident, even if it meant being separated from her sisters. But her adoptive parents had always held her at arm's length, and Tabitha had yearned to feel like part of a real family for as long as she could remember.

And now she was. The twins were everything to her. What more could she possibly want?

She shifted the SUV into Park and gathered her purse, phone and diaper bag before climbing out of the car. It always took three separate trips to unload everyone and everything after an outing, so she left the windows unrolled. The twins slept soundly while a spring breeze ruffled their soft, downy hair.

Tabitha had just finished fiddling with her key ring and grabbing hold of the house key when she looked up and saw a man sitting on her front steps.

"Oh." She stopped dead in her tracks.

Was she seeing things? Why was there a stranger on her porch? And why was he wearing a black Stetson pulled down low to cover his face?

Tabitha's heart thudded so hard and fast that she

couldn't breathe. The diaper bag slid from her shoulder and fell to the ground with a thud.

West.

No. It couldn't be. That was impossible. Lots of men wore cowboy hats around here. This was Texas, after all.

She blinked hard, squared her shoulders and marched forward. But her hands trembled so badly that her keys jangled like church bells.

"Can I help you?" she managed to sputter.

That hat…that sculpted jawline…those impossibly broad shoulders. They were all so familiar that Tabitha wanted to drop everything, sprint toward the stranger and throw herself into his arms.

Thankfully, she still had enough sense to realize she shouldn't. *Couldn't.* Dead ex-fiancés just didn't appear from thin air and pop up out of nowhere. She hadn't somehow conjured the father of her children simply because she'd been thinking about him. Tabitha didn't know what was going on, exactly, but one thing was certain. Whoever this man was, he wasn't West Fortune.

But then he lifted his head and aimed his attention squarely at her. His eyes were covered with sunglasses. Aviators, like West had always worn. And even though Tabitha couldn't see past the dark lenses, she could feel his stare. It burned into her with the heat of a thousand Texas summers.

Everything seemed to move in slow motion as the man stood and walked toward her. Tabitha felt like she was looking at him through a long, dark tunnel.

Her head went fuzzy, and she couldn't hear anything but her pulse throbbing in her ears. Thump, thump, thump. Then he removed the sunglasses, his gaze collided with hers and Tabitha's knees turned to water.

"Hi there, darlin'." His voice was quiet. Tender. And his expression bore only a ghost of a smile.

It was him.

How?

Why?

What was *happening*?

"West?" she breathed, and then the whole world tilted sideways as she slunk to the pavement.

Chapter Two

West sent up a silent prayer of thanks that he managed to catch Tabitha just before she hit the ground. As many times as he'd imagined this homecoming... *longed* for it...he'd never envisioned it involving a near-concussion.

Hadn't he hurt Tabitha enough already?

Idiot. He cursed himself. In hindsight, he should've figured out a gentler way to break the news of his "resurrection." But how? He'd gone straight to Tabitha's house the second he'd crossed the town border into Chatelaine. West didn't want to risk anyone else seeing him—not even his family. Tabitha deserved to hear the truth from him and him alone, to see for herself that he was really alive...

Even if she might not love him anymore.

"West?" She blinked up at him as he cradled her head in his hands. They were sprawled in the middle of the sidewalk that led up to her quaint little porch and, Chatelaine being Chatelaine, their dramatic reunion hadn't gone unnoticed.

Across the street, Betty Lawford paused from trimming her rosebushes to sneak a sideways glance at

West as he helped Tabitha to her feet. She squinted at him, and he waited a beat too long to avert his gaze. Betty's mouth dropped open and her gardening shears slipped from her gloved hands.

Cue the small-town rumor mill in three...two... one...

"Let's get you inside, darlin'," he whispered into Tabitha's ear.

A lock of her wavy blond hair tickled his cheek, and the sweet familiarity of her honeysuckle scent nearly brought him to his knees. He'd never forgotten that scent—not even once in all the time he'd been away. For nineteen long months, West had closed his eyes and tried to conjure it up late at night when loneliness wrapped itself around him, as thick as a blanket. All he'd wanted was to come home. Not just to Chatelaine...to West, *home* still meant Tabitha.

It always would.

"I'm fine," Tabitha said as she scrambled to her feet, but the tremor in her voice betrayed her. "I just..."

She looked up at him. *Really* looked, and the tears that pooled in her eyes made West's gut churn in a way that was far more painful than any damage the man who'd been hell-bent on destroying him could've done.

"Come on, now. Don't cry." He cupped her elbow and steered her toward the house, stepping gently over her bags, still strewn on the sidewalk.

Had she been on a trip somewhere? Her handbag looked like it had grown three sizes since he'd been gone, and she'd also been carrying a bulky duffel bag—baby blue, covered with little teddy bears doing cartwheels.

"Here, let me," West said, taking the keys from her hands and unlocking the front door.

Tabitha stepped inside and lingered in the front entrance as if in a daze. Then she reached a shaky hand toward him and placed it on his chest, right over West's pounding heart.

A smile blossomed on her lips. "You're really here. It's you."

"It's me." *Not a ghost and not a dead man.* West's throat grew thick. He'd waited so long for this day, and in his lowest moments, he'd feared it might never come. There was so much to say, but now that he was here, he didn't even know where to start.

Start with "I still love you." How about that?

He rested a hand on top of hers, still pressed against his heartbeat. "Tabitha, I—"

"The babies!" she blurted, eyes going wide.

West had been so wrapped up in what he'd been about to say that it took a beat for her words to sink in. Even then, they still didn't make sense. "The what?"

"The kids are still in the car. I was going to unload everything first and then go get them, but then you, well…" Her face flushed. West was guessing "you came back from the dead" sounded too ridiculous to utter aloud. "I need to go get them."

She brushed past him, headed back out the door toward her car, still parked at the curb with the windows unrolled. West narrowed his gaze at the backseat and could just make out two tiny blond heads and the headrests of two bulky car seats. His heart sank all the way down to the soles of his custom-made, leather Lucchese boots—one of the few remaining vestiges of his former life that he still owned.

Tabitha has children?

He wasn't sure why he was surprised. She'd made her feelings clear during her big breakup speech. Tabitha wanted a family. She wanted kids and a white picket fence and all the things that West hadn't been able to promise her. Of course she'd moved on.

His gaze flitted around the living room, hungry for details. But there wasn't a family photo in sight, so he blew out a breath and forced himself to walk back outside where Tabitha was unbuckling one of the seat belts and talking to the kids in a singsongy voice that made his heart feel like it was being squeezed in a vise.

"Here, hold Zane for a minute. I'll go get Zach." She placed a baby into his arms.

"Um…" West stiffened.

"Seriously?" Tabitha's eyes flashed. "He's a baby, not a porcupine. You'll be fine holding him for half a second."

Across the street, Betty Lawford had given up any pretense of clipping her roses and was now watching with unabashed interest as she watered her sidewalk with a garden hose.

The baby stared up at him and made a happy gurgling sound as he reached for West's Stetson with a pudgy fist.

"Oh, no you don't, buddy." A smile tugged at his lips,

and he relaxed a little as he readjusted his grip on the child.

The tiny thing was as light as a feather and had a sweet little dimple in his chin, like the one West's brother Camden had when he was a kid. And suddenly, he was drowning in grief—grief for what he'd lost when he'd been away, grief for everything he'd willingly given up when he'd told Tabitha he never wanted to be a father, grief for the long "dead" West Fortune.

Because he wasn't that guy anymore. That life was buried and gone, as evidenced by the fact that he was now holding a baby who belonged to Tabitha and another man. His stomach tightened, and he looked away, focusing on some random spot in the distance, above the boy's head.

"Are you coming, or has holding an infant rendered you paralyzed?"

West snapped his head toward the porch, where Tabitha stood glaring at him with the other baby balanced on her hip.

"We're coming," he said and somehow managed to gather her previously discarded bags in one hand without dropping the tyke in the other as he made his way back to the house.

It wasn't as if West disliked babies. They were fine. Wonderful, even. So long as they belonged to someone else. West's upbringing had been far too tumultuous for him to believe he could ever be a decent father. His parents had made one another miserable for West's entire childhood. There'd been cheating on both sides and so much screaming that West routinely fell asleep at night with his head buried under his pillow and his hands clamped over his ears.

He didn't know what he would've done without his two brothers, Camden and Bear. Bear was only a year older than him, but when West was particularly upset or scared, Bear would crawl into his bed and tell him an adventure story to distract him. Kids shouldn't have to rely on their siblings for a sense of stability, though. Somewhere deep down, West was messed up. When his parents were killed in a plane crash five years ago, he'd hoped he could finally shake the bad memories and learn to let it all go. But after he asked Tabitha to marry him and she'd started talking about kids, he'd gotten a sick feeling in the pit of his stomach every time the subject came up. How could he possibly have a family of his own when all his memories of childhood were so tied up with misery? West wouldn't know the first thing about building a happy home for an innocent child like the one in his arms.

By the time he stepped inside the house, Tabitha had already settled Zach on a blanket in the center of the living room with a collection of brightly colored stackable cups. The baby attempted to stick one of them inside another as Tabitha plucked Zane from West's arms as if rescuing the child from some mortal danger.

That was on him, he supposed. He'd never given Tabitha any reason to believe he was good with children. Because he *wasn't*. West didn't have the first clue what to do with a baby.

That was probably beside the point, though. He still had plenty of explaining to do, and he wanted to get it done and get out of here before Tabitha's husband came home. Chatelaine was a small town. He'd have to meet the man eventually, but not yet. Not today. Not until he'd had a little time to come to grips with this painful new reality.

Would time really help, though? If the past year and a half had taught West anything, it was that he'd never stop loving Tabitha, no matter how many days, months...*years*...slipped by.

"I'm sorry," he said quietly. "I shouldn't have just shown up like this, out of nowhere. But when I got word that it was safe to come back, this was the only place I wanted to be. Here...with you."

Tabitha's expression softened, but there was still a wariness about her that hit him square in the heart. "I don't understand, West. Everyone thinks Trey Mendez shot and killed you."

In his capacity as lead county prosecutor, West had been responsible for putting Mendez in prison three years ago. He'd worked on that trial night and day for weeks. The defendant had been a high-profile member of a Mexican drug cartel responsible for bringing large amounts of narcotics and other illegal contraband across the border. It had been the most important win of his entire legal career.

And then, the same day that Tabitha had broken off their engagement, Mendez's shady lawyer had managed to get his client released on a technicality.

"It was in all the papers, West. Witnesses saw you get shot. There was a *funeral*." Tabitha's voice broke on that last word, and something inside him broke along with it.

He swallowed hard.

"Mendez shot me—that much is true." West rolled his shoulder. He still had some residual stiffness and intermittent pain from the gunshot wound. He'd been lucky, though. An inch to the left, and the bullet would've hit his subclavian artery, and there would've been no need to fake his death. His demise would've been one hundred percent real. "You probably know this already from the news coverage, but it happened on the riverbank near the Fortune ranch. I'd gone out there to think things over after you and I...well...anyway, Mendez found me there the following morning. He shot me from far off, near the back side of the ranch, where the drop into the river is at its highest point. After I fell backward into the water, I stayed under long enough to convince him I was dead."

West's body had never been recovered, obviously. But he'd emptied his pockets of all his personal effects, hoping they'd wash up onto the shore. A fisherman found them in a shallow creek the following morning, and Trey Mendez was caught and convicted almost immediately. But his ties to the cartel ran deep. West knew better than to show his face until the man was dead and gone. So he'd hunkered down and stitched himself up with a needle and thread and a bottle of good whiskey. Then he'd found a job on a ranch and gone underground.

She shook her head, as if she couldn't believe what he was saying. "But I still don't understand. Why didn't you come home once you were safe?"

"He threatened you, Tabs. He said he was going to kill 'my pretty fiancée' to get back at me for getting him put away. The only way to keep you safe was to let him, and everyone else, think I was dead." West had given up his life to save her, and he'd do it again in a heartbeat. No matter what the cost.

Tabitha wrapped her arms around herself, and her bottom lip began to tremble. "But we were…"

Broken up.

Neither of them wanted to say it, but the truth hung over them anyway, stealing all the oxygen from the room.

West took a deep, ragged inhale. "I know, but it didn't matter, Tabs. Mendez wouldn't have believed it. He would've thought I was lying just to keep you safe."

One of the twins let loose with a stream of baby talk, and Tabitha blinked, as if waking up from a trance.

Her head snapped toward the windows facing her quaint, shady street. "Where is Trey Mendez now? You don't think he's coming here, do you? The children—"

West rested his hands on her shoulders, and even that simple contact was almost enough to bring him to his knees. It had been so long since he'd touched her, kissed her, loved her. And yet being this close to her was like muscle memory. Every part of him remembered what it felt like to hold Tabitha Buckingham in his arms.

"They're safe. You all are, I promise," he said with an undeniable ache in his tone. "Mendez died in prison this morning. As soon as I got word, I came straight here."

Home. That's what he'd meant to say. *As soon as*

I got word, I came straight home. The instant West found out it was safe, he'd come back to the only home he'd been dreaming of since he'd been away. At least he'd caught himself before he'd said so out loud.

This was another man's home, not his.

"It's all over, Tabs. You've got nothing to fear now." His gaze cut toward the twin boys, playing with their toys, clumsily stacking the cups with their little pudgy hands. Why did it hurt so much to look at them? "Your kids are safe. Everything's okay."

Was it, though? A world where Tabitha's heart belonged to someone else didn't seem like it would ever feel okay.

He didn't have a choice in the matter, however. While he'd been stuck biding his time, the world had moved on without him. He'd have been a fool to expect otherwise, especially when he'd let Tabitha walk away without a fight.

Regret burrowed deep as he took in her familiar features. She looked exactly the same. Same light blond hair, same sparkling blue irises—the exact color of the wild bluebonnets that blossomed across Texas every spring, transforming the landscape into a sea of dusty blue-violet that stretched out all the way to the horizon. It was going to take him some time to come to grips with the fact that even though things might look the same, deep down in his soul, everything had changed while he'd been gone.

But then Tabitha's graceful fingers toyed with the gold chain around her neck, and she absently fiddled with whatever charm or pendant hung from the delicate necklace as she seemed to do her best to absorb everything he'd just told her. West glanced at her hand, fluttering as nervously as a bird searching for a place to land. And that's when he saw it...

The ring. *His* ring—the one that had been crafted from gold from the Fortune family mine. The one he'd hidden in a box of chocolate the day he'd asked her to be his wife.

Hope welled in his heart as he lifted his gaze slowly to meet Tabitha's, and for a tender, breathtaking moment, their eyes met. The present suddenly looked and felt a lot more like the past, and West could almost breathe again. She still wore his ring. That had to mean something, didn't it? Then one of the babies started babbling again, and the moment turned bittersweet.

Confusion gripped him, rooting him to the spot, even as a part of him felt inexplicably drawn to the boys. He studied the dimple in Zane's chin. *Just like Camden.* Then West went numb all over as he realized Zach had one too.

He glanced back at Tabitha, searching her gaze for the answer he was in no way prepared to hear.

"West." The smile she offered him was so steeped in vulnerability that he felt it deep in the pit of his stomach. "Meet your twin sons."

"My *sons*?" West swayed slightly on his feet, and Tabitha was almost glad she wasn't the only one who'd just experienced the shock of a lifetime.

Her ex-fiancé had just *come back from the dead*. Was she living in a soap opera now, or had the loneliness she sometimes battled late at night finally become so intense that she'd started hallucinating? Those seemed like the only two options. West had explained what happened, but she still couldn't seem to reconcile his version of events with the reality she'd been struggling to accept for the past year and a half. So much loss. So much grief...grief so thick that if she hadn't had the twins to worry about, she might have let it consume her.

The boys had saved her. Once Tabitha found out she was pregnant, she had a reason to get out of bed in the mornings. She hadn't been at all sure how she would do it all on her own, but knowing she would soon have two tiny, helpless babies to take care of was enough to help her put one foot in front of the other. So that's what she'd done. Day after day after day...until slowly, the twins became her whole world and West became her past.

Except now that past was standing right in front of her, shell-shocked to discover that he was a father.

"Yes, Zach and Zane. They're turning one year old in just a few weeks." She bustled toward the boys, trying her best to tamp down the urge to throw herself protectively in front of them. But that was crazy, right? West was their daddy, and he was a good man.

A good man who told you he never wanted children, she told herself. As if she could've forgotten that devastating little nugget.

She sat down cross-legged on the blanket and pulled the twins into her lap, facing West, and ran a hand over each of their downy heads. "This one is Zane and this one's Zach."

West came closer, lowering himself down in front of the boys. He reached out a hand and Zach grabbed hold of it, balling West's finger into his little fist. Zane let out a squeal.

A look of wonder splashed across her ex-fiancé's face for a beat, replaced quickly by bewilderment as he swiveled his gaze back and forth between his sons. "Are they identical?"

Tabitha laughed, despite the absurdity of the situation. "You're not seeing double. Yes, they're identical."

"Identical twins." He gave his head a little shake. "Wow."

"Yeah. It's kind of crazy, isn't it?" She nodded, remembering the afternoon she'd found out she was carrying twins.

It had been an appointment for a routine sonogram early in her pregnancy. She'd expected to come home with a blurry image of West's baby to tack to the front of her refrigerator with a magnet. Instead, the doctor had grinned widely at her and asked if she was ready for the surprise of her life. Afterward, she'd gone out for ice cream with her sisters and smiled so much that her cheeks were sore by the time she finished her three scoops of mint chocolate chip. A moment of pure joy amid so much darkness.

"Can I hold them?" West asked. The uncertainty in his gruff tone just about broke Tabitha's heart.

"West, they're your children. You don't need to ask permission." She didn't know where they went from

here, but she'd never try and keep the twins away from
their father. They could figure things out, even if they
were no longer together.

Because the fact of the matter was, they *were* still
broken up. Just because West wasn't really dead didn't
mean they were back together. Tabitha had ended their
engagement when he'd told her he didn't want children, but there was so much more to it. She'd played
second fiddle to his career for a long, long time, and
it was his job as a county prosecutor that had landed
them in this terrible mess. Tabitha couldn't pretend
otherwise, no matter how very badly she wanted to.

You need to protect your heart, she reminded herself as she all but melted at the sight of West gathering the two small boys in his arms. Never in her life
did she think she'd witness a moment like this one. It
felt like a gift straight from heaven.

"West, I'm so sorry about everything that happened
to you. It must have been so hard to leave everyone
and everything you knew behind." For *her*. He'd done
it for her. Tabitha was still so mad at him for so many
things, but that one truth threatened to make her want
to sweep them all under the rug.

Still, couldn't he have somehow sent her a message
to let her know he was alive?

Her stomach squirmed. *What part of broken up
don't you understand?*

"I'm the one who's sorry." West shook his head.
"You've been taking care of two babies all on your
own."

"Not completely alone. Lily and Haley have been a

huge help. They were even my birthing coaches. Can you believe it?" She smiled, proud of all the progress she and her sisters had made on their relationship. Tabitha had wanted to be close to Lily and Haley since she'd first learned she had birth sisters.

But West's smile went sad around the edges. He hadn't been there for the birth of his children, and no matter where they went from here, nothing would ever change that.

Tabitha was suddenly exhausted. This was all too much to take in, especially the painful, overriding truth of this heart-wrenching homecoming: West was back, but he didn't want to be a dad. He'd said so himself.

You're still on your own in this, and don't you forget it.

"I should get the twins down for their nap," she said as the boys began to fuss.

"Okay, I'll help." West stood, a twin tucked into the crook of each arm. "Lead the way to the nursery?"

Who was this man, and what had he done with the real West Fortune?

Tabitha swallowed around the lump lodged in her throat and showed him the boys' room with its whimsical elephant mural she and her sisters had painted during the pregnancy. The nursery was a small, modest affair, just like the rest of the house, but what it lacked in space it more than made up for in warmth and coziness. The whole room was decorated in soothing shades of blue. A rocking chair stood by the window, and among the stuffed animals lined up on the bookshelves, sat a framed photo of West.

His gaze snagged on it just as they finished getting the babies situated in their side-by-side cribs. He looked at it for a long moment, and when he turned back toward Tabitha, she was almost certain she saw tears in his eyes.

"I can't believe these precious wonders are mine," he whispered. "They're perfect, Tabs."

She bit down hard on the inside of her cheek to keep herself from crying. He was really and truly here, and he was saying all the right things. The urge to throw herself into his arms and kiss the stuffing out of him was almost too much to bear.

"Can I ask you something?" he murmured, shifting closer to cup her cheek in one of his big, warm palms.

Wild horses couldn't have made her turn away. "Ask me anything. I'm sure you have a lot of questions."

"We both do. That's why I think it's best if I stay here for a while." He moved the pad of his thumb gently over the side of her face.

"In Chatelaine?" Tabitha swallowed. Where else would he go? West was a legend in this town.

But that wasn't what he'd meant, and they both knew it.

"Here with you and the boys. Let me stay, Tabs. Please? The thought of you is what kept me going the past nineteen months. Your beautiful face, what we had together... I know there've been ups and downs, but you're everything to me."

"West, we can't just—" Tabitha shook her head, desperately needing to think. She couldn't automatically jump back into a relationship with both feet. It wasn't just the two of them anymore. She had the boys to think about.

"You broke my heart," she finally said, because it was the truth, and she couldn't just forget it had ever happened. When she'd ended the engagement, he'd told her maybe it was for the best. He hadn't even put up a fight.

"I know I did. I know, sweetheart. And I know I have a lot to prove now that I'm back." A muscle ticked in his jaw. "All I'm asking for is a chance to show you how different things can be, and a chance to get to know my kids. Children were never part of my plans, but they're here now. And now that I *am* a dad, I want to be the kind of father these little angels deserve. My life is starting over, and this is the only place I want to be." He aimed a purposeful look at the babies, tiny chests rising and falling in a sleepy rhythm. "Right here, with all three of you."

"What about your work?" She wiped a tear from her cheek. "Will you go back?"

She wasn't even sure why she asked. Even if he said no, she knew she couldn't trust it. That job had meant the world to him.

"I don't know." He shook his head and sighed. At least he was being honest. She had to give him credit for that. "The only thing I'm sure about right now is that I want to be a good dad. Let me stay. Please? Even if it's just for a little while."

It was everything Tabitha had wanted to hear two years ago, but so much had changed since then. How could she possibly believe him?

"This house is too small for four people, even when two of them are babies." Tabitha glanced toward the living room and her resistance wavered…ever so slightly. "You'd have to sleep on the sofa. Understood?"

"Understood." He beamed at her, and butterflies took flight in her belly, just like they did back when things were simpler.

Back before West had died and come back to life. Back before they'd become parents. Back before he'd broken her heart into a million pieces.

That battle-weary heart of hers clenched, reminding her that it was little more than scar tissue now. She had no intention of giving it away again. Not to West, or anyone else. Not ever.

Tabitha smiled through her tears.

What did I just agree to?

Chapter Three

The following morning, West watched the sun come up as he sipped a cup of coffee on Tabitha's front porch. He'd been up for hours already.

The sofa was plenty comfortable. He had no complaints about that whatsoever. But he'd been working as a ranch hand for the past year and a half on a huge cattle farm out in West Texas, doing the kind of manual labor he hadn't done since he'd been a teenager. Life in the saddle started before sunrise, and West's body hadn't gotten the message that he was home now with his head resting on a soft pillow in Tabitha Buckingham's cottage in Chatelaine instead of sleeping in a bunkhouse with a dozen other cowboys.

Even if he'd been able to instantly adjust to his new surroundings, West wouldn't have gotten more than a few fleeting hours of shut-eye. His mind couldn't stop spinning.

Twins.

His boys slept just down the hall. He was a *father*. He'd come home to reclaim his life, only to find that that life looked completely different than the one he'd left behind. His heart was full to bursting in a way that he'd never dreamed possible.

West drained his coffee cup, eyes trained on Betty Lawford's roses across the street. The colorful blooms seemed brighter than they'd been yesterday. His gaze drifted upward. And the soft pink sky over Chatelaine felt more expansive than ever. It was a whole new world, and even though West had a long way to go to earn his place in it, his heart stirred with hope. The West Texas ranch belonged to another lifetime—one that he had no intention of returning to ever again.

He went back inside the house, moving as quietly as he could in his sock feet, Wranglers and a plain white tee. His first order of business when he'd gotten up had been a phone call to his brother Camden, which had been full of yet more surprises. He'd put off telling his family he was really alive until he'd gotten a chance to see Tabitha face-to-face. As much as he loved the Fortunes, he hadn't wanted to risk Tabitha hearing he'd faked his own death from someone else. Now that he'd had coffee and put the sofa back together, he wanted to try and get the twins changed and ready for the day before she woke up. No time like the present to start acting like a real, hands-on dad.

The boys were both stirring quietly in their cribs when West entered the nursery. Their big blue eyes swiveled toward him, and he held his breath, worried they might burst into tears at the sight of a stranger. A father suddenly appearing out of nowhere couldn't be easy on a kid, even an infant. But one of the babies smiled, then the other. They pulled themselves up and reached plump arms toward him, eager to be held.

The sweet moment quickly descended into chaos. West had never changed a single diaper in his life, let alone two. But he somehow managed to get both boys cleaned up and dressed in soft, baby-blue onesies by the time Tabitha entered the room.

"Good morning," she said in a singsong voice as she tied the sash of her bathrobe into a knot, nearly plowing straight into West in the process.

"Oh. You're up already." She stumbled to a halt, gaze flitting from the baby powder spread liberally all over the carpet to the pile of discarded diapers beside the changing table.

"It took me a few tries to figure out how the self-adhesive tape on these things works," West admitted, patting Zane's tiny bottom. The baby was nestled in his arms, while Zach did a little dance in his crib and babbled at his mama. Trying to hold both of them at the same time first thing in the morning had proved more challenging than wrestling an alligator. "And I was aiming to get everything cleaned up before you got up. I just…"

"But you got the twins changed and dressed? All by yourself?" Tabitha was staring at him as if he'd sprouted another head overnight and already placed a black Stetson on top of it.

"I guess I did." He gave the baby in his arms a crooked smile. "We figured it out, didn't we, Zane?"

Tabitha let out a quiet laugh.

"What?"

She shook her head. "It's nothing. You did a great job, West."

"Something's funny. Come on now, darlin'," he said, and her cheeks went pink at the endearment. He supposed he was going to have to stop talking to her like he used to...like she was still his. Old habits died hard, though. Especially when those habits had been the subject of his every fantasy for the past year and a half. "Tell me."

She bit back a smile, eyes flitting toward the twin propped in the crook of his elbow. "That's not Zane. It's Zach."

So much for nailing the fatherhood thing.

"Oh."

"Don't let it take the wind out of your sails. You did great," Tabitha said, graciously ignoring the explosion of baby powder and the wad of discarded diapers.

West blew out a breath. What kind of dad couldn't tell his own children apart? Not a good one, that's for sure.

"Trust me. It's an easy mistake to make." She laid a hand on his forearm, and the moment her fingertips brushed against his bare skin, she shivered.

Then she jerked her hand away and pasted on a nervous smile.

West crumbled inside. The sight of her obvious discomfort around him was almost as upsetting as the fact that he couldn't tell which twin was Zach and which one was Zane.

"When was the last time you made that mistake?" he asked, arching a brow at her.

Her hand fluttered to her throat. *"Me?"*

West nodded. "Yep."

"A while." She swallowed, and West traced the movement up and down the slender column of her throat. "But I'm with the boys every day. Don't be too hard on yourself. You'll learn, West."

Would he, though? Or was he doomed to make the same mistakes his parents had made when he'd been a child? The past had a tendency to repeat itself. Shame washed over him at the very thought of it.

You're not your father. You're here *now.*

"What time did you get up?" Tabitha asked as she pulled her robe more tightly around herself.

He hated that she felt so nervous around him. Absolutely despised it. "I got up a few hours ago. Couldn't help it. Days started early back on the ranch."

Her forehead puckered. "The ranch?"

They still had so much to talk about, so much to say. And yet somehow none of it seemed important compared to the two little lives he was now responsible for.

"When I was in hiding, I worked as a ranch hand on a place out in West Texas," he said.

"I see. I guess that explains the tan." Her gaze flitted to his biceps, and her flush grew a deeper shade of pink. "And the muscles."

"Baling hay and working with cattle will do that."

"I suppose that was quite a change from working as a prosecutor." Tabitha cleared her throat, and her gaze sharpened the way it always did when the subject of his job came up.

She had every right to be upset about his career

and what it had done to their relationship, now more than ever.

West nodded. "Indeed."

Tabitha brushed past him to lift Zane from his crib. The child cooed and let out a stream of baby talk that sounded an awful lot like *mama*.

"Mamamammammma." Zane's little face split into a wide grin, showing off his four teeth.

West could only stare in wonder. "Did he just say mama?"

"Sort of." Tabitha moved her hand over the infant's slender back in soothing circles. "They both started saying it a few months ago. Their very first word."

"That's...amazing." West's throat went tight. He knew better than to ask if they could say *dada*. They had no reason at all to know that word.

"Do you want to help me feed the boys breakfast?" Tabitha asked, throwing him a bone.

He nodded. "Yes, please. I'd love that."

West studied every move she made as she sliced up a banana, cooked two helpings of breakfast cereal and scrambled an egg on the stove. Then he helped get the boys settled in their highchairs and clipped bibs around their necks, wiped chins and did the airplane food thing with tiny spoons and forks.

The sheer amount of effort it took to take care of the twins' most basic needs was overwhelming. By noon, West was more exhausted than from a full day in the saddle.

She's been doing this all on her own for nearly a year.

He wasn't sure how it would be possible to make

everything up to Tabitha, but he was determined to give it his best shot.

"I should get some work done. I have a few clients waiting on new website designs." Tabitha gestured toward her laptop, sitting atop a small table off to the side of the kitchen after they'd gotten the twins down for their afternoon nap. "Have you thought about contacting your family and letting them know you're back?"

West scrubbed the back of his neck. "I did that first thing this morning. I called Camden, and once he got over the shock of hearing from me, he got me caught up on everything that's been going on with the Fortunes."

Tabitha shot him a knowing grin. "You're not the only one with a surprise up your sleeve."

Of course she knew. Chatelaine was a small town. No one could keep a secret here—all the more reason he'd had to go into hiding.

"So have you met this mysterious 'step-granny' of mine who managed to get nearly all of Elias and Edgar Fortune's grandchildren to pick up and move here to Chatelaine?"

According to Camden, the only holdout was their other brother Barrington, more commonly known as "Bear." Thus far, Bear had refused to respond to the cryptic email that had been sent to all the grandchildren from a woman purporting to be the widow of their long-lost grandfather Elias Fortune. The woman had summoned all six of Elias and Edgar's grandchildren to Chatelaine to settle Elias's estate.

The other Fortune grandchildren—those of Edgar and Elias's brothers Walter and Wendell—had been notably left out. While Edgar and Elias had a reputation as the black sheep of the family, Walter and Wendell were the golden boys. Quite literally. Back in the 1950s, they'd struck gold in West Texas. Given Elias and Edgar's penchant for getting into trouble, they'd kept their successful mine a secret, leaving the headstrong brothers to mine for silver in Chatelaine. That venture had ended in disaster—the great Chatelaine mine collapse in 1965. Fifty miners had lost their lives.

Walter had since passed on, and Wendell had settled right here under the alias Martin Smith. But he'd recently been outed as Wendell Fortune, the owner of Fortune's Castle in Chatelaine, the epicenter of all the current family drama.

West hadn't been altogether surprised that Bear was avoiding the current situation in Chatelaine. Elias had fallen off the map years ago, after the collapse of the Fortune family silver mine. No one had heard from him in decades, much less known that he'd passed away and left a widow behind. Still, the fact that no one seemed to know Bear's whereabouts made his radio silence for the past three months somewhat concerning. Bear wasn't the best with correspondence, but after what West had been through, he needed to know that every member of his family was safe and sound.

He'd need to deal with that sooner, rather than later. It ranked right up there with *learn how to be a father* on his to-do list.

"Have I met Freya Fortune?" Tabitha nodded. "Of course. Since she gathered everyone up and got them here to Chatelaine, all your relatives found out about the twins. Everyone has been great about keeping in touch and sending baby gifts. I know they're all going to be so happy to hear you're alive, West. But you should probably prepare yourself. I have a feeling your homecoming is going to be a tad overwhelming."

As if anything could trump learning that he was a dad to twins.

West opened his mouth to respond, but before he could get a word out, there was a soft knock on Tabitha's front door.

She stiffened. "Are you expecting someone?"

"Tabs, I told you not to worry. We're safe." West's gut churned. The woman he loved didn't feel safe in her own home, and it was all his fault. "I promise."

She nodded. "The past twenty-four hours have just been a lot. Whoever that is, let's just hope they don't wake the boys."

Tabitha hurried to the door, and West came to stand behind her. Through the door's double-pane window, he spied an older woman with a stylish ash-blond haircut with bangs. At first he thought it might be Betty Lawford from across the street, bringing by a casserole or something as a guise for satisfying her curiosity about West's sudden reappearance. But this woman was no Betty Lawford, in her trademark housecoat and curlers. Whoever this was, she was dressed to the nines in a crisp white blouse with a wide, turned-up collar and slim black trousers. West was pretty sure her gold *H* belt buckle was designer.

"You wanted to know more about your mysterious step-granny. Well, here's your chance." Tabitha's gaze shifted toward West. He knew exactly what the sudden sparkle in her eyes meant. *I told you to prepare yourself, cowboy.* "It's Freya Fortune."

"Fresh squeezed lemonade." Tabitha set a tray containing three frosty glasses on the coffee table in her crowded living room. If she'd known a guest was coming, she probably would've picked up the twins' play blanket and toys.

She *definitely* would've put away the folded quilt and stack of pillows currently sitting at the foot of the couch, broadcasting the fact that West had spent the night there.

She pasted a smile on her face and pretended nothing was amiss, despite the way Freya's left eyebrow ticked skyward when she'd first noticed the neatly folded bedding. "From my lemon tree in the backyard."

"How nice. Thank you so much, Tabitha," Freya said.

Tabitha sat down beside West on the sofa, thighs pressed together since the blanket and pillows occupied a good deal of space. She didn't dare move them, lest she draw more attention to their presence. West's family had no idea they'd broken up before he went missing. Like everyone else in Chatelaine, the last thing they'd expect was for Tabitha to have him sleep on the sofa after finding out he wasn't really dead. For all they knew, West was simply her long-lost fiancé and the father of her children. Why wouldn't she welcome him back with open arms, right into her life?

And her bed.

Tabitha couldn't even think about going to bed with

West right now. Scratch that: in reality, she'd thought of little else in the past twenty-four hours. Which was a problem. A *big* one.

She snuck a sideways glance at him as he picked up one of the glasses of lemonade and offered it to Freya, sitting across from them in one of Tabitha's shabby chic floral chintz armchairs. The scales probably tipped more toward the shabby side than chic, but she'd done her best to make a cozy, happy home for her and the boys. When her adoptive parents found out she was pregnant with twins, they'd reacted by throwing money at her. It was their go-to solution for dealing with problems of any and all variety.

Tabitha had insisted she didn't need their financial help. What she wanted most was for her mom and dad to act like normal grandparents and shower the boys with affection. To spoil them with love instead of expensive gifts and offers to buy the three of them a big new house.

That wasn't the Buckingham way, though. Her parents weren't neglectful or cruel. Tabitha had lacked for nothing growing up. She'd just never felt like she truly belonged in their high-society world of country clubs, private schools and children who were raised by nannies instead of their mothers. So it hadn't been much of a surprise when she'd found out she'd been born into an entirely different family. She'd been a *triplet*!

Tabitha probably shouldn't have been surprised she'd ended up with twins. Multiple births ran in families. But the last thing she'd expected after becoming a pseudo-widow was to see a pair of little pink lines on the pregnancy test she'd taken solely to convince herself that the nausea and exhaustion she'd been experiencing since West's sudden death were part of the grieving process.

The surprises just kept on coming, didn't they? The biggest shock of all was sitting right beside her, looking as manly and rugged as ever—and very much *alive*—among all her vintage, romantic decor.

Why, oh why, did he have to look so good? The old West Fortune had always made her go weak in the knees, but this new version of West was almost too much to resist. The physical work he'd been doing while in hiding showed. His T-shirt strained across his firm back and chest. The weariness he'd carried in the lines around his eyes while he'd been a prosecutor had all but disappeared. For as long as Tabitha had known West, there'd been a restlessness about him that always made her feel like a part of his mind was always someplace else. But now he seemed as still and solid as a rock.

Or maybe, after changing an average of one hundred forty diapers a week for the past year, she was just a sucker for a man who seemed dead set on figuring out how to be a hands-on dad.

You can't trust that, and you know it. The twins are a novelty to him. Once he goes back to work, he won't have time to play house anymore.

He was simply telling her what he knew she wanted to hear. West had always been good at that. He could charm the skin off a rattlesnake. It was part of what made him so good in front of a jury.

Tabitha dragged her gaze away from West's cattle-wrangling biceps and forced herself to pay attention to whatever Freya was saying.

"Again, I'm so sorry for turning up out of the blue like this. I came as soon as I heard the news." The older woman paused to take a sip of her lemonade.

"Well, it's a pleasure to meet you, ma'am," West said with a nod.

Freya waved a hand. "Oh, honey. There's no need to *ma'am* me. We're family."

"So I hear." He rolled his left shoulder— a new habit he'd developed in his absence.

"I'm not sure what all Camden and Tabitha have told you, so I'll just start at the beginning. A few months ago, your grandaddy, Elias Fortune, got very sick and fell into a coma. I'm sorry to say he never recovered. As you know, he'd been away from Chatelaine for a long, long time. After the silver mine collapsed all those years ago, he left and never looked back. The memories were just too painful."

West nodded, his expression inscrutable.

Freya's version of past events was more than a tad sugar-coated. Everyone in town knew that Elias and his brother Edgar had been at least partially responsible for the tragedy at the mine. They'd blamed the foreman, who'd died in the collapse, along with forty-nine other miners. Then they'd quietly left town to start over in Cave Creek, where a new generation of Fortunes had been born. But Elias and Edgar soon skipped town yet again, and from there, no one knew what had become of Elias.

Until Freya showed up, that is.

"Your granddaddy left a Last Will and Testament, and I'm here in Chatelaine to make sure his final wishes come to fruition. He left everything to you, your siblings and your cousins, West." Freya paused, toying with the silver bangle bracelets on her wrist. "For a very specific purpose."

West glanced at Tabitha. She'd heard about the terms of Elias's will from her sister Lily, who was married to West's cousin Asa. But this was Freya's moment, not hers.

The older woman took a deep breath. "Elias wanted to make amends for all the wrongs he and his brother bestowed on the Fortunes, so he left instructions for his assets to be used to make each of your wishes come true."

West's brow furrowed. "I'm not following."

"I'm here to do as your granddaddy spelled out in his will. In order to do that, I just need to know one thing." Freya's eyes glittered. "What's your most fervent wish?"

"My most fervent wish," West echoed.

"Yes. Just say the word, and I'll see to it that your granddaddy grants it from the grave." Freya threw up her hands. "You've been gone quite a while, West. I'm sure there are plenty of things you need. A new house where you and your sweet family can start over, perhaps?"

Tabitha flew to her feet. "I should check on the twins."

She couldn't stay here and listen to this anymore.

Shouldn't. This was personal Fortune family business, and despite what everyone still thought, Tabitha wasn't West's family. He was the father of her children, but that's where their connection ended. Full stop.

And the fact that she had no idea how he would answer Freya's question wasn't lost on her. Once upon a time, she knew everything about West Fortune. Those days were over, though. She didn't have a clue what he wanted anymore. They'd been living completely separate lives for nearly two years. Time and circumstances had changed Tabitha so much that she was a whole new person now. A *mother.* It would've been ridiculously naive to think that West had remained exactly the same.

Then why won't you give him another chance?

The thought made her breath catch in a way that was equal parts tempting and terrifying. She pushed it away before it took root.

"I just heard one of the babies cry," she blurted.

"I didn't hear anything," Freya countered.

West eyed her with concern. "Are you okay, sweetheart?"

I'm not your sweetheart. She felt empty inside, hollowed out by grief. She'd felt this way for so long that she no longer knew how to fill up that emptiness with something good and pure—something that might just be within arm's reach. If only she could believe.

"I'm fine." A bald-faced lie. "Like I said, I need to check on the boys. You two visit for a while."

Once she'd excused herself, Tabitha fled to the comforting familiarity of the nursery. The boys were still fast asleep, so she sat down in the rocking chair all on her own, wrapped a knitted throw over her shoulders and quietly rocked back and forth. The motion of the chair helped calm the jumble of thoughts and emotions that had her so tied up in knots. She'd been a mess since she'd found West waiting for her on her front porch yesterday. It felt good to do something normal again—something she'd done a million times before.

Whenever Tabitha felt overwhelmed or couldn't sleep at night, she came here and sat in the dark with the twins. Just being near them kept her grounded and reminded her what was truly important. So long as her boys were safe and sound, everything was okay in her world. She could deal with the rest in due time.

But she hadn't had a second to catch her breath since West's return. He was *right there*, all the time. Before their breakup and before his disappearance, she would've given anything to have so much quality time with the man she loved. Now, it was just confusing.

Had she done the right thing when she'd ended their engagement?

She wasn't sure anymore. In all the months he'd been gone, she'd never once wavered on this point. As much as she'd missed him and mourned his loss, she knew she'd made the right choice. West hadn't wanted a family and he hadn't made her a priority in his life. Not truly.

Things seemed so different now. But Tabitha wondered how long it would last.

She closed her eyes and dropped her head against the back of the rocker. Thanks to the tiny size of her living quarters, West's deep voice carried from the other room. Was there nowhere she could go to escape the man?

"My most fervent wish? That's easy. I don't even have to think about it."

Tabitha stopped rocking and strained to hear more, even though it mortified her to her very core that she was so invested in his answer.

"I want to be a good dad," he said, voice firm with conviction.

Tabitha's throat closed as he went on.

"It's so strange. I never wanted kids...could never imagine it. But the instant I learned those boys were mine, I felt bonded to them. Like I'd give my life for them. Is that crazy?"

"That's not crazy at all, West. That's love," Freya said, and Tabitha could hear the smile in her voice, even from the other room. "And that's exactly why I know you'll succeed in being a great father."

"Thank you for saying that, but you don't even know me."

"I know enough. Trust me, just being here counts for a lot. That's what children want most—your nurturing presence. Shower them with warmth and affection, and you can't go wrong. You'll learn the rest along the way."

There was the unmistakable sound of boots against the hardwood floors, which meant West had stood up. Apparently, the visit was winding to a close.

His voice grew quieter as they moved toward the front door. "This advice is just the thing I needed to

hear. You know, Freya, for someone who doesn't have
kids, you sure are knowledgeable about parenthood."

"Your granddaddy and I weren't blessed with children, but I had a daughter a long time ago. It feels like a
different life now. We grew estranged, and it's the single biggest regret I've ever had," Freya confessed, and
the sadness in her tone brought a tear to Tabitha's eye.

She froze, unable to even wipe it away. Freya had
a daughter?

"I'm sorry to hear that," West said.

"It's water under the bridge, but don't you worry.
We both know you won't be making that mistake."
The front door swung open on squeaky hinges, but
still she couldn't bring herself to move. "Tell Tabitha
thank you for the lemonade, and I'll come back soon
so I can give those two babies of yours a squeeze."

Tabitha's throat closed up tight. Her eyes burned
from the effort it took not to break down and cry.

Why couldn't she have Freya's unshakeable trust in
West? He wanted to be a good father. It was his most
fervent wish, and this time he hadn't said it just for
Tabitha's benefit. Freya had offered him a *house*, and
still all he could talk about was how much he loved
Zach and Zane.

Before yesterday, if someone would've told her that
West was really alive and he was coming home, her
reaction would've been pure, unparalleled joy. But seeing him again stirred up so many conflicting feelings,
especially when he'd jumped to the immediate assump-
tion that she'd moved on with someone else. He'd seri-

ously thought she'd married another man and started a family!

How was she supposed to wrap her mind around that?

Tabitha sighed. The man sleeping on her couch was the West she'd fallen in love with, but at the same time, he was also a complete and total stranger.

Even so, maybe it was time to take him at his word.

Chapter Four

Later that evening, Tabitha didn't know what to do with herself while West single-handedly got the twins dressed in their pajama onesies and read them a bedtime story. Once again, he got the boys mixed up and accidentally dressed Zane in the onesie that had Zach's name embroidered across the chest. But other than that tiny mistake, he did a great job.

"You don't need to hover," he told her as he re-dressed the babies in the correctly monogrammed pajamas. "I've got this."

She lingered in the doorway to the nursery for a beat, but finally went to the kitchen to pour herself a glass of wine once West was settled in the rocker with the twins balanced on his lap and a picture book in his hands.

He was their dad. She needed to let him figure some things out on his own, just the way she'd done after she'd first brought them home from the hospital. It was part of the bonding process. West had already missed out on so much. She knew she needed to give him some time and space with the boys on his own so he could get to know them. It was just so hard when she was accustomed to doing it all by herself. Day after day...

"Success! They're both down for the count." West raked a hand through his hair as he joined her in the living room. When his gaze landed on the laptop balanced on a pillow on her lap, a furrow formed between his brows. "You're working?"

Tabitha nodded. "Yes, but I'm just finishing up. Since I had a little bit of free time, I wanted to catch up on a website I've been building for a new florist in San Antonio."

"I don't know how you can think straight at this hour." He shook his head and came to sit beside her on the sofa.

"It's only eight o'clock." She closed the laptop and set it on the coffee table beside her glass of wine and the baby monitor, although the square footage of her cottage pretty much made the second item unnecessary.

"Right, and between the twins and your job, you've been going nonstop all day. If I had to read a legal brief right now, I wouldn't be able to make a lick of sense of it." He dropped his head on the back of the sofa and blew out a breath.

"West Fortune, are you saying that two sweet, almost-one-year-olds are harder to take care of than an entire ranch full of horses and cattle? Because that's definitely my takeaway from this discussion." She gave him a playful poke in the ribs.

He grabbed hold of her index finger before she could snatch it back, and before she realized what was happening, they were casually holding hands...as if doing so was normal. As if they were a regular married couple who'd just put their babies down for the night.

"That's precisely what I'm saying." West turned her hand over in his and stared for a beat at her bare ring finger.

Her engagement ring still hung from the gold chain around her neck. She couldn't bring herself to remove it. Hiding it away in her jewelry box seemed wrong, and yet sliding it back onto her finger didn't make sense either. West was back, but they were still stuck in some strange romantic limbo. Tabitha couldn't seem to figure out whether she should take a step forward or backward. Both options felt equally terrifying.

West's gaze shifted from their linked hands to her face, and his expression turned so achingly tender that her mouth went dry. "I'm here now. You don't have to do it all anymore. Let me help, Tabs."

"I'm trying," she said, but it was so much easier said than done. Couldn't he see that?

She'd worked hard at building this life. It was simple, and yes, it was exhausting at times. But it was *hers*. She'd made a happy home for herself and her boys without any financial assistance from her parents or any full-time help. When West had been presumed dead and she'd found out she was pregnant, Tabitha had felt like the ground had suddenly disappeared from beneath her feet. She didn't know how she'd ever manage things on her own.

But like the good, strong Texas girl that she was, she'd pulled herself up by her bootstraps and become the best mom she could possibly be. Her twins were healthy and happy. Her bank balance was modest, but she'd managed to stash away enough savings for emergencies and create a business from scratch where she could be her own boss and work from home around her children's schedules.

"What are you so afraid of?" West asked softly, and the pad of his thumb began to move in slow, gentle circles over her palm, soothing her before she could protest and pretend she wasn't scared.

The truth was she was terrified to her very core. Once she let this man in, there was no going back. She couldn't go through losing him. Not again. She'd barely survived it the first time around.

"I just need some time, okay? This is all a lot. My head hasn't stopped spinning since you showed up on my front porch yesterday."

"That's fair." West nodded and squeezed her hand so tight that she thought he might never let go. "But tell me something. It's been hours since Freya left. Are you going to tell me what's been going on in that pretty head of yours all day, or am I going to have to guess?"

West still knew her well enough to know when she was overthinking something.

Tabitha could remember a time when he had told her that one of the most important aspects of his job as a prosecutor was being adept at studying human behavior. To know when witnesses were lying and when they were being truthful, to be able to tell when they actually remembered something and when their subconscious was merely filling in the gaps, to know when to push someone into talking and when to back off. But the way he'd always been able to see her inside and out was uncanny sometimes. She'd thought that after so much time apart, he'd no longer be able to read her like a book.

Wrong.

"Did you mean what you said when she asked you about your most fervent wish?" she asked, because she just didn't have it in her to try and hide the truth. What was the point?

"Why, Tabitha Buckingham." West's eyes went wide in mock astonishment. "Were you eavesdropping on my private conversation with my step-granny and widow to my long-lost grandfather?"

She loved that he could still make her laugh, even when the ground beneath her feet had started to feel so shaky again. "A little bit, yes."

"I meant every word." The smile on West's lips faded, and suddenly he was looking at her with such earnestness that she couldn't remember how to breathe. "But I understand why it's hard for you to believe that, sweetheart. All I'm asking is for a chance to show you how much you and those boys mean to me. I know it won't happen overnight, but that's okay. We have all the time in the world now."

Did they?

Because it didn't feel that way. He'd been gone so long that a part of Tabitha wanted to consume him completely, just to make up for lost time. Tomorrow wasn't a promise or a guarantee. She'd lost enough people in the course of her lifetime to have that truth engraved on her heart from now until the end of time.

Maybe that's why, instead of pulling her hand away and going to bed—*alone*—like she should have, Tabitha did the one thing she couldn't stop thinking about. She shifted to sit in his lap, wrapped her arms around his neck and kissed West Fortune with every pent-up ounce of longing that she'd been trying her level best to pretend she didn't feel. And it was such a relief to let it out, to pour all of her grief and need straight into the only man who'd ever held her heart, that she couldn't seem to stop—not even when her fingers found their way to the buttons on West's shirt. Not even when he groaned into her mouth as her hands slid over his bare chest. And *especially* not even when he picked her up, carried her to the bedroom and kicked the door shut with the heel of his boot.

A shiver coursed through her as he lifted her dress over her head. West hadn't seen her like this in so long. She'd given birth to two children since they'd last slept together, and she half expected him to look at her like she was a stranger. But instead, his gaze landed on the chain around her neck and the gold ring resting against her heart.

His lips curved into a tender smile, and he hooked a fingertip in the chain to reel her in for a kiss.

Tonight wasn't a pledge or a promise. West had said so himself just a few minutes ago. This moment was something else entirely—it was about remembering. Remembering who they both were and what they'd meant to each other, once upon a time. It was about rewriting the last two years and finding that elusive happy-ever-after. Not for tomorrow, but for yesterday.

For those two innocent souls who'd once been on the verge of standing before God and promising to love, honor and cherish each other til death do them part.

Tabitha missed the people they'd been back then— back before work had begun to consume West and things had spiraled so wildly out of control. Everything had been so simple once upon a time. So pure.

So she closed her eyes, returned West's kiss and did her best to fall into yesterday.

West didn't want to open his eyes the following morning. Somehow he knew if he did, the magic spell that he and Tabitha had managed to weave the night before would be broken in the cold light of day. Sure enough, once he dragged his eyelids open, he found himself alone in Tabitha's bed. The sheets beside him were cool to the touch, and her pillow barely had the slightest indentation.

Who knew how long he'd been lying there by himself?

He sat up and scrubbed a hand over his face. This wasn't good. He'd taken things as slow as possible last night and tried his hardest to follow Tabitha's lead. But she'd been in such a rush. He'd never felt as though they'd really connected. Every time he'd tried to pull back and meet her gaze, she closed her eyes. When he'd whispered sweet nothings in her ear, he hadn't been sure he'd actually gotten through to her. It almost felt as if she'd been somewhere else entirely instead of the here and now, with *him*, in this place where he'd hoped they could build a new beginning.

When he got up and left the bedroom, he found her already dressed and put together in the kitchen, even though the twins were still sleeping soundly in the nursery. She had a mountain of fruit on the counter in front of her, along with a line of plastic containers with lids, and seemed to be in the process of meal planning for the twins for what looked like an entire year. Possibly the rest of their lives.

"Good morning," she said, focusing intently on the mango on her cutting board instead of looking him in the eye. "Sorry if I woke you. I couldn't sleep."

West surveyed the countertop and arched a brow. "I can see that."

"Can I get you a cup of coffee or something? A banana, maybe?" She held up a piece of fruit, and as soon as their eyes locked, her bottom lip began to quiver. Just the tiniest bit. If West had blinked, he would've missed it.

He took the banana and set it back down on the counter. "Thanks, but no. Talk to me, sweetheart. What's really going on here? You seem upset."

She took a deep breath. "I'm not upset. I'm just…"

"This is about last night, isn't it?" West asked, stating the obvious. If he'd done something wrong, he wanted to know about it. Losing his life had humbled him every which way, and he didn't want anything coming between them again. Not if he could help it.

"I'm not ready for this." She gestured to the empty space between them, which felt impossibly big all of a sudden. Like a wide, endless cavern. "I thought I might be, but I'm not."

"I understand," he said quietly.

It's going to be okay. You just got back. There's still time to be a family together. Just because she's not ready now *doesn't mean she'll never be ready.*

At least they'd had last night. It had been so good to hold her again, to love her. It hadn't been perfect, but that didn't matter. And now, the memory of it gave West a glimmer of hope that they could somehow find each other again.

"Last night was a mistake," Tabitha said, and he wasn't altogether sure if she was trying to convince him or herself.

Either way, he died a little bit inside. *Please don't say that. Loving you would never be a mistake.*

"I see." He nodded. His mouth had gone dry as a bone. He needed coffee…or water…or to just go back to sleep and convince himself that this conversation wasn't really happening. That it was all just a bad dream.

It wasn't, though. It was as real as all those long, lonely months he'd spent on the run. He'd finally come home, and somehow, he still hadn't made it all the way back.

West knew he had no one to blame but himself. He'd been the one to push Tabitha away when she'd started talking about children. She'd wanted it all—the white picket fence, lemonade stands on hot summer days and pony rides during rodeo season. And she'd had every right to expect it, because they'd been engaged to be married. But as the wedding date grew closer, it had all started to feel impossibly real. He had no business raising kids. What if he ruined them? What if history repeated itself and he screwed everything up, just like his parents had?

The shame of his childhood crept in until it was overwhelming, and instead of sharing those thoughts and fears with his beautiful fiancée, he'd pushed her away. He'd thrown himself into work, because that was what he was best at—putting bad guys away. It was honorable and meant that West was a good man. A man who was nothing like his dad.

Did it, however? Look where it had gotten them.

"It's okay, Tabs. Really. I just want to be in your lives, no matter the terms. I'm not going anywhere. You have my word." He reached for her hand and squeezed it tight. "I'll go back to staying on the couch. If you still want to let me stay, that is?"

His heart was in his throat. What if she said no?

She lifted her chin and gazed up at him, and for a moment, West was convinced she was about to send him packing. But then the twins began stirring in the nursery. Happy, gurgling baby sounds drifted toward them from the hallway.

Tabitha's eyes went soft, and the space between them felt less daunting. She was right there again, just an arm's length away. Close enough to touch, to kiss, to love.

"Of course you can stay. The boys would like that very much." She smiled and West felt it down to his soul. "So would I."

At least she still wore his ring on the chain around her neck. The thin band glimmered in the sunshine streaming through the kitchen window. Like liquid gold, like hope itself.

This wasn't a happy-ever-after, and it might never be. Tomorrow was full of unknowns, as West knew all too well.

But it just might be a start.

Chapter Five

Tabitha had to tell her sisters about West. Or maybe she simply had to get out of the house. She hadn't set foot out in the real world since her twins' dad had turned up out of the blue, and things had begun feeling much too cozy. Too much like a family, which they weren't.

Which was probably why she'd let down her guard last night.

No more. She'd woken up feeling intensely vulnerable in West's arms in the wee hours of the night. Was she really going to give him the chance to break her heart again? She couldn't. It was too soon, and she couldn't trust whatever she was feeling for him again. It had only been two days, for goodness' sake. Anyone could throw themselves into fatherhood and family life for forty-eight hours.

After the painfully awkward morning-after conversation, Tabitha sent an urgent text to her sisters and all but fled to the Cowgirl Café to meet Lily and Haley, who'd dropped everything they were doing and come straight to the restaurant while West stayed home with the twins.

Having the sort of freedom for an impromptu girls' lunch in the middle of the day was a novelty that Tabitha was in no way accustomed to. Under normal circumstances, it would've thrilled her to pieces. But there was no world in which her current circumstances would've been described as normal. She'd left *normal* behind the very instant her dead ex-fiancé had tipped his Stetson and called her "darlin'."

"So what's the big emergency?" Lily plucked a fry from the enormous platter of chili fries in the center of the table, gaze swiveling between Tabitha and their other sister, Haley.

"Don't look at me. Your guess is as good as mine." Haley shrugged one slender shoulder and reached for her cherry Coke. "Tabs, is everything okay? And where are the twins? I thought your babysitter had to quit because of the cheer squad."

"She did. The boys are actually with—um—" *With their daddy. You know, the love of my life, who we all thought was dead.* She couldn't just blurt it out like that, although the temptation was real. It might be nice not being the most flabbergasted person in the room for a change.

"They're fine," she said simply, resting her hands on the table. She stared longingly at the chili cheese fries. The Cowgirl Café in downtown Chatelaine never disappointed. Tabitha and her sisters had been regulars since the restaurant's recent grand opening, so summoning them here with a text message had seemed like a good idea earlier this morning.

But the establishment was owned by Bea Fortune,

one of West's cousins. Tabitha hadn't seen Bea bustling around the restaurant yet, but she was bound to turn up sooner or later. If Freya had already heard about West's return, the rest of the Fortunes had to know too. It was a wonder the gossip hadn't reached her sisters yet. The chili cheese fries could wait. She needed to go ahead and drop the bomb before someone else did.

"Tabitha, you wouldn't believe what I overheard Betty Lawford saying this morning while I was at GreatStore buying a dog bed for Max." Lily jammed a fry into a pile of chili in a way that could only be described as aggressive. "I was *livid*."

Haley held up a hand. "Wait. You bought Max *another* dog bed? Didn't Asa already buy one…or three?"

"Yes, but now Max has gotten accustomed to having one in nearly every room at the ranch. I figured another one couldn't hurt." Lily bit her lip. Tabitha would've bet good money she'd purchased more than just the one bed. Lily worshipped her sweet new rescue dog and vice versa. "Anyway, that's not the point. Just as I walked past the gardening aisle, I overheard your neighbor telling someone that she'd seen West. *West Fortune!* Can you believe it. She tried to say she'd spied him alive and well and drinking coffee on your front porch this morning."

Tabitha nearly choked on her Dr Pepper. The bomb had already been dropped, apparently.

"I set her straight right away. That kind of talk is just hurtful. The past two years have been hard enough without subjecting you to false hope," Lily huffed.

"Oh my gosh, what is wrong with people? Tabs, just

ignore that nosy busybody." Haley's forehead scrunched and her drink paused en route to her mouth. "But wait. Was there really a man drinking coffee on your front porch this morning?"

Guilty as charged.

Listen to her. Even her internal thoughts were starting to sound like something West would say in a courtroom. He'd been back in her life less than forty-eight hours, and everything was changing. Was it really so bad that she just wanted this crazy ride to stop for a second so she could get off and catch her breath?

"As a matter of fact, there *was* a man on my porch this morning." Tabitha took a deep breath. "And that man was indeed West Fortune."

A chili-laden fry fell from Lily's hand and landed on the table with a splat.

Haley blinked. "I don't understand."

That makes two of us. Tabitha could still barely wrap her head around it herself.

She spent the next few minutes getting her sisters caught up while the untouched chili fries grew cold and the chili congealed. No one cared about food anymore. West Fortune was *back from the dead*.

"This is amazing! I just can't believe it. I'm so, so happy for you, Tabs." Lily reached across the table to take both of Tabitha's hands in hers.

That was what did it. Her sister's kind words seemed to reach deep into Tabitha's chest and tear her heart in two as easily as if it were made of paper. A sob escaped her and then another, until she was reduced to a bawling wreck right there in the Cowgirl Café among the bandana-style napkins and mod Western decor.

Haley gently dabbed Tabitha's face with one of the aforementioned napkins. "Tabs, what's wrong? West coming home is a good thing."

"I know it is. It's just a little…*overwhelming*. That's all." She lowered her voice until it was barely above a whisper. "We were broken up, remember? But now he's back, and somehow it doesn't feel that way. It almost feels like we're still engaged to be married."

"Maybe this could be your second chance." Lily's eyes sparkled.

Haley smiled in such a hopeful way that Tabitha's heart wrenched. "Do you think things between you might work out?"

"To be honest, I'm not sure there's an us anymore." Why did things seem so uncertain in the light of day? When it was just the two of them, Tabitha could almost imagine a future with West. But the moment the real world crept in, so did her doubts. Case in point: this morning. "He told me he was adamant about not wanting kids before, but you should see him with the boys. He's trying really hard to be a devoted father. It's all so bewildering."

"I'm sure it is, but does it have to be? All that really matters is how you two feel about each other." Lily squeezed Tabitha's hands so hard that her knuckles turned white, which only made her more emotional. All Tabitha had wanted since she first learned she was a triplet was to feel close to her sisters. She just never imagined it would take a soap-opera-level crisis in her personal life to get there.

"You still love him," Haley said. A statement, not a question.

"I do, and I know he loves me too." Tabitha closed her eyes against the memory of West's crestfallen expression this morning when she'd told him that sleeping together had been a mistake. Trying to force the image away didn't do any good at all. The devastated look on his face was seared into her mind's eye for all eternity. "But the choice to be a dad wasn't his. I keep thinking about what might happen once everything settles down and life goes back to normal."

"I think the lesson from all of this is that we never know what might happen in the future, but you shouldn't rule out the possibility that you and West can work things out," Haley murmured.

Lily nodded. "That's right. The only thing you can do is take things one day at a time."

One day at a time. Tabitha took a shuddering inhale. She could do that, couldn't she? West had waited nineteen long months to come home, never losing faith that it would happen someday. What must that have been like, knowing that everyone he loved had gone on with their lives thinking he was dead? Had he read his obituary in the *Chatelaine Daily News*? Had he imagined the funeral and all the tears shed by his loved ones? After West's death and subsequently learning she was carrying his babies, Tabitha's grief had been suffocating. It had been like losing the love of her life all over again, only this time the loss was permanent. Crushing.

But she'd only lost West. West had lost everything and everyone he'd ever loved, all in one fell swoop.

Tabitha couldn't imagine living a day in his shoes when he'd been in hiding. He must've grieved the loss of West Fortune as fervently as everyone else had.

If he could hold out hope indefinitely, never knowing when he could come home, surely she could learn to take things one day at a time. They'd leapt in with both feet last night, and look how that had turned out. No wonder things had been so awkward and she'd felt so vulnerable. She'd acted as if the past two years had never happened, as if she and West were the same people they'd been before they'd broken up and he had been forced to go into hiding.

They weren't the same people. The old Tabitha Buckingham was as much a part of history as the old West Fortune. Her sisters were right. Before they could move forward, they needed to get to know each other again.

Baby steps, Tabitha told herself. Just like Zach and Zane learning to balance on their precious little feet. After all, they were the most important part of this equation. The twins were everything. If she and West were ever truly going to be together again, they'd do so as a family. White picket fence and all, just like Tabitha had always dreamed of...

Which was exactly the sort of happy-ever-after fantasy that had torn them apart the first time around.

* * *

West headed straight to his brother Camden's ranch after Tabitha returned home from lunch with her sisters. If she needed space, he was determined to give it to her. They'd rushed things last night. He knew that now, and he couldn't afford to make that kind of mistake again.

He'd spent the past two years in a race against time. Waiting, waiting, waiting...never knowing when it would be safe to come back home. A day hadn't passed without West knowing precisely how long he'd been away.

But now time was back on his side. There was no more need to worry about the passing minutes, days, weeks...*years*. Still, he couldn't help feeling like he had to make up for lost time. He wanted his life back, damn it. Every lost, lonely second of it. When Tabitha kissed him last night, every last remaining shred of his patience had crumbled. He'd actually been fool enough to believe that all their problems had vanished the moment he'd crossed the Chatelaine town border.

It's going to be fine, he told himself again. Whatever Tabitha needed, he'd do it. They could get past this. They had to.

He took a deep breath as he lingered on the front porch of Camden's ranch house and looked around. His brother had done well for himself. The aptly named Chatelaine Ranch was located off the highway, down a long dirt road that led to the shady, somewhat secluded property. West had driven past the ranch offices when he'd first arrived and then various buildings earmarked for the equestrian riding camp and school his brother was working on getting started. The ranch house sat by itself on the back side of the property, overlooking a wide green pasture.

Before he had a chance to knock, the door swung open.

"Well, aren't you a sight for sore eyes?" Camden said as he wrapped West in a big bear hug. "Welcome home, brother."

"It's good to be back. More than a bit surreal, but good."

Camden pulled back to look him up and down. "You look good, man. Less lawyer and more cowboy. It suits you."

"You think?" West pulled his black Stetson down lower over his eyes.

"Okay, so the hat isn't new. But the tan from being in the saddle all day certainly is. And your Wranglers are a fair bit more worn-in than they used to be. If you're not careful, I'll put you to work here at the ranch. I'm always looking for good help." Camden winked.

"Don't tempt me with a good time," West said.

In a way, those days at the ranch out in West Texas had been a blessing. The work had been physically demanding enough that he hadn't had the time or energy to dwell on his circumstances. It wasn't until the lights went out at the bunkhouse every night that his mind wandered back to Chatelaine. Then he'd fall into a deep sleep and dream of sultry nights in South Texas. Of Tabitha. Of home.

He couldn't work as a ranch hand here in Chatelaine, obviously. He was an attorney, and the whole point of coming home was to get his life back. West just hadn't allowed himself to dwell on that part yet, seeing as his job had been a point of contention between him and Tabitha. Now more than ever before, seeing as it had been the entire reason he'd been forced to go into hiding.

"Nice place you've got here, Cam." West nodded toward the paddock where a pair of glossy chestnut quarter horses grazed.

"You want a tour?"

"I'd love one."

His brother showed him around the ranch, from the main house to the barn, the stables and beyond. Afterward, they settled on the broad back porch of the ranch house with ice-cold bottles of beer.

Camden couldn't seem to stop stealing glances at West and grinning from ear to ear. "Man, it's so good to see you. I still can't believe it. You're *alive*."

"And I'm a *dad*." West took a long pull of his beer. "But I suppose I don't need to tell you that. I'm the last one to know."

"Twins." Camden let out a low laugh. "I bet that was a surprise."

"You have no idea." Sometimes he still couldn't believe it, even after the two or three dozen diaper changes he'd racked up since he'd been back. At least he'd figured out which side was the front of the darn things and which side was the back. Now he just needed to master the fine art of telling his children apart. "It was a good one, though. The best news I've ever heard."

"Was it?" Camden arched an eyebrow beneath the brim of his cowboy hat. "As I recall, you've always felt a bit ambivalent about fatherhood. Not that I blame you. Our parents weren't exactly the poster couple for parenthood."

"Not at all." West gave his brother a tight smile. There was no need to get into specifics. They both remembered the slamming doors and screaming fights that punctuated their childhoods on a regular basis. Try as he might, West couldn't forget those dark days, and he knew Camden well enough to realize neither could he.

Kids shouldn't be forced to be part of a family dynamic like that. Innocent children deserved better, which was why West was determined to be a better man than his father was. No matter what it took.

"And you're right. Kids were never part of the plan, but now that they're here..." West sighed. He just couldn't put the feeling in words, no matter how hard he tried. "I love them. I don't have a clue what I'm doing when it comes to taking care of them, but I do love them."

Camden's green eyes went soft. "That's all that matters, bro. You'll figure out the rest. After all, you've dealt with some of the worst criminals in the state of Texas. Twin one-year-olds have got to seem easy by comparison."

West snorted. "You'd be surprised."

Camden shook his head and laughed. "Do you have any idea how grateful I am to see you again?"

"I think I've got a good idea." West's heart swelled. He had more to be grateful for than he deserved.

"Especially with Bear falling off the face of the earth and all. I've missed my brothers, man. I finally got a text from him two days ago and all it said was that he'd try and get to Chatelaine soon. That he's got 'a lot going on.'" Camden made finger quotes around that last part.

He and West exchanged a glance. *Yeah, here too.*

"Does he know about me yet?" West drained what was left of his beer.

"Not yet. I needed to see it myself to believe it." Camden pulled his phone from the back pocket of his Wranglers. "I'll text him right now. I'd call but we both know he'd never answer."

He tapped out a message and within seconds, Camden's phone chimed with an incoming text.

"It's him. Wonders never cease. If I'd known that all it took to get him to communicate was a resurrection, I would've tried to arrange for one sooner," Camden said, squinting at the screen. "He says to tell you he's happy you're alive, and he'll come to Chatelaine before the end of the month. That's a promise."

West nodded. "Good. It'll be great to see him again, and he's got a lot to catch up on around here."

Surprise twins, West back from the dead, Freya Fortune turning up out of nowhere and their grandfather's eccentric Last Will and Testament. What next? Amnesia?

Camden tapped the neck of his beer bottle against the one in West's hand. "Ain't that the truth."

Chapter Six

The following morning, West paid a visit to the local law enforcement offices. He'd been dragging his feet on coming face-to-face with the sheriff since he still wasn't sure what to do about his career prospects, but as a former officer of the court, he had a duty to explain how a man who'd been declared legally dead had turned up alive. He couldn't keep putting it off, especially now that word was beginning to spread.

"Well, as I live and breathe." Sheriff Cooper's eyes lit up the second West strode into his office. He removed his feet—clad, as always, in worn brown leather cowboy boots—from his desk and stood. "So the rumors are true. You're really alive."

"Looks that way, doesn't it?" West removed his hat and extended his hand for a shake, but the older man came around the front of his desk and pulled him into a hug instead. He pounded hard on West's back, as if proving to himself that West wasn't merely a ghostly apparition.

"Do you have any idea how much we've missed you around here?" the sheriff said, eyes crinkling in the corners. "I cried like a baby when I heard that you were back from the dead. It's like a miracle, son. Tell me everything."

So West did. He took a seat and explained what had happened on the day Trey Mendez found him on the riverbank, how he'd faked his death and left just enough personal possessions behind to convince the outlaw he'd truly been murdered. The sheriff listened, riveted, until West finished.

Then he let out a long, low whistle and sat back in his chair. "Like I said, a miracle."

"Let's hope the state bar agrees," West said. Without a law license, he couldn't work. As nice and quiet as the past few days had been, he had twins to provide for now. Tabitha had been doing it on her own for far too long.

That was going to change. The rest of their future was still undetermined, but West was adamant about making parenthood easier on Tabitha.

"Don't you worry about the state bar." Sheriff Cooper waved a hand as if batting away a pesky insect. "Our office will help you get the legalities straightened out as quickly as possible. Chatelaine still needs you, West. *We* need you. When can you come back to work?"

And there it was—the very question West had been trying to avoid.

"You mean as a staff attorney or something, right? I'm sure the county prosecutor position has been filled." West couldn't imagine his job being kept open for so long. It just wasn't possible.

"Oh, no. I mean head honcho, just like before.

We've had an interim county prosecutor since your disappearance. There was no reason to keep your desk vacant, but you left some pretty big shoes to fill, West. We've been searching for a fully qualified candidate for quite some time. You're not an easy prosecutor to replace. As fate would have it, the perfect person for the job just walked into my office and is sitting right across from me." The sheriff shot finger guns at West.

Message received. The job was still his if he wanted it.

West cleared his throat. "I don't know, Sheriff. I appreciate the offer. You know I do, but it's a lot to think about. I just got back, and my life isn't as simple as it used to be."

"Ah, right. The twins." Sheriff Cooper flashed him a smile. "How are the little rug rats doing? Their first birthday has got to be coming up soon, right?"

West swallowed and a wave of shame instantly engulfed him. He knew the twins were almost a year old, but he had no idea what their actual birthday was. Father of the year material, he was not.

"I, um…" He shook his head.

The sheriff averted his gaze, and the easy, breezy vibe of their conversation shifted as the older man graciously made excuses for West's obvious cluelessness. "Well, like you said, your life isn't quite as simple as it used to be. I'm sure there's a lot to catch up on."

It was more kindness than West deserved, at least in his own estimation.

"You know what we need?" Sheriff Cooper eyed the desk pad calendar that took up the majority of the wooden surface of his desk. "A party."

He slammed his palm down on the calendar for added emphasis.

"A birthday party?" West asked, still thinking about the twins and their upcoming milestone.

"No." The sheriff shook his head and then shrugged. "Well, yes. That, too. But that's your department. I'm talking about a party for you."

Out came the finger guns again.

West shifted uncomfortably in his chair. "That's really not necessary."

"On the contrary. It's *very* necessary. You're a bona fide town hero, West. And after everything that's happened, now you're a Chatelaine *legend*. Let the community give you a proper welcome home, son. I insist."

West tried to beg off. "I really don't think…"

"Stop." Sheriff Cooper held up a hand. "Consider it done. We'll have a picnic party in the park and invite the entire town. You've made a tremendous sacrifice for the good of Chatelaine. It's the very least we can do. Does this Saturday work for you?"

West tried to imagine the look on Tabitha's face when he went home and told her the sheriff was throwing him a literal party. She'd assume he'd already agreed to go back to work as the county prosecutor, no matter how fervently he denied it. This couldn't end well.

"Good. It's settled, then," the sheriff said, mistaking West's silence for agreement. "Saturday, it is. Make sure you bring those sweet boys of yours. And Tabitha, too, of course."

Right, because nearly everyone in Chatelaine thought they were still engaged, West's former boss included.

Now wasn't the time to set the record straight on that matter. His life was already front-page news. And he wanted to protect Tabitha and the twins from as much of that attention as possible.

"Of course," West echoed.

What else could he say?

"We'll be there with bells on."

Tabitha took a deep breath as she pushed the twins' double stroller up one of Chatelaine Park's shaded walking paths late Saturday afternoon.

She thought she'd been prepared for this. A welcome-home picnic in the park sounded thoughtful and sweet. Was she thrilled that it had been Sheriff Cooper's idea? Not exactly. The man worshipped the ground West walked on and she had no doubt that he'd move heaven and earth to get West back to work as the county prosecutor. Still, it was a lovely gesture, so when West had come home from the sheriff's office the other day and told her about the party, she'd ignored the warning bells going off in the back of her head and told him she was happy for him. Of course she'd attend the picnic with him, and the boys would come too. It would be just the sort of family outing she'd always dreamed about.

Or so she'd thought.

"Wow." She blinked at the massive banner strung from two of the park's tallest trees. *Welcome home, West Fortune!* The lettering on the banner was so big that it could probably be seen from space. "This is really something, isn't it?"

West's gaze shifted to the white tent that had been

assembled beneath the banner, complete with a podium and enough balloons to send the entire setup airborne. His forehead crinkled. "I guess Sheriff Cooper wasn't kidding when he said he wanted the whole town to come out for this."

"Apparently not." Tabitha pasted on a smile. This day was about West, not her. He deserved to be welcomed back to Chatelaine with open arms, even if this "picnic" was more along the lines of a state fair than a simple small-town party in the park. "I'm happy for you. Chatelaine loves you, West. Our town is a safe place to live and raise a family, largely because of you. It's good that the community appreciates all the hard work you've done on behalf of the county."

"Thank you for saying that." He wrapped an arm around her shoulders and pressed a chaste kiss to her forehead.

A ridiculous shiver coursed through her. They'd been tiptoeing around each other the past few days, pretending their night together had never happened, but her body betrayed her at even the most casual contact.

"But this doesn't mean I'm going back to work as the county prosecutor," he said.

Tabitha nodded. "I know. You mentioned that already. A few times, actually."

The furrow in West's brow deepened. "Tabs, I—"

Before he could finish whatever he wanted to say, Sheriff Cooper came bustling down the path toward them.

"The man of the hour is here! And you've brought

your beautiful family. Look at how much those twins have grown." He gave West a one-armed hug before leaning in to kiss Tabitha on the cheek. "I'm so happy for the two of you. I know you're even happier than the rest of us to have West home, as fit as a fiddle."

"The boys and I are thrilled," Tabitha concurred.

"Good, good. Now we just need to get your man back to work. Chatelaine needs him." The sheriff shot her an exaggerated wink. "Maybe you can help me twist his arm and get him to take his old job back."

Her stomach instantly hardened. Why did she get the feeling that there was more to this party than a simple welcome home?

West swooped in with a reply, saving her from having to stumble through an awkward response. "Now, now. This is a picnic, isn't it? No work talk."

Sheriff Cooper held up his hands. "Okay, okay. I'll try to keep a lid on any more job offers. But come Monday, look out. In the meantime, come with me, West. You've got to see the spread we've got set up over by the tent. Hot dogs, with all the fixings. Big ole slices of watermelon. It's like the Fourth of July." He held a finger to his lips. "Don't tell anyone, but we might have some fireworks planned over the lake tonight."

Fireworks? Tabitha thought she might be sick. This was definitely more than just a picnic. It was a full-on parade, with maybe a touch of bribery thrown in for good measure. The county courthouse was probably rolling out a red carpet for West right this very second. He'd never be able to resist this kind of star treatment. Who would?

"You don't mind if I borrow West for just a minute, do you?" The sheriff didn't wait for an answer. He threw an arm around West's shoulders and hauled him away, toward the festivities.

West held up a hand in a parting wave, and Zane and Zach waved back at him from their stroller.

"Dddddddada," Zane said, his pudgy little hand flailing wildly. And then, more clearly, "Da-da."

"Dada," Zach echoed. "Dada, dada, dada."

Tabitha gasped and knelt down beside the stroller. "That's right, boys! Dada. There's your daddy!"

She waved alongside them, and her heart leapt straight to her throat. They'd just called West daddy... and he'd missed it, because he was busy being courted by the sheriff.

It wasn't West's fault, obviously. He could've just as easily been leaving to go to GreatStore or Camden's ranch. And it wasn't like he was going to live on her sofa and be a stay-at-home dad for the rest of their lives. Eventually, he'd be going back to work somewhere. If the sheriff wanted to give him his old job back, it only made sense to accept the offer. West loved that job.

Still, the idea of the man she loved going back to prosecuting criminals made Tabitha's stomach churn. It wasn't just the fact that his long work hours and his tendency to become consumed with his trial work had been a point of contention between them. That job had put West in harm's way. Tabitha, too. What if he prosecuted another psychopath who ended up getting off on some sort of technicality and the bad guy came after Zach and Zane?

A chill wracked through her at the very thought.

"Tabitha, are you okay? You look like you've seen a ghost." Lily came jogging toward Tabitha on the walking path with her dog Max scampering alongside her.

Not a ghost. Just a glimpse of what our future might be like if West goes back to work saving the world. How many times could one man come back from the dead?

She stood, cleared her throat and tried to push away her anxiety. West had point-blank told her that he hadn't accepted the sheriff's offer...yet. "Fine. I was just surprised, that's all. The boys just said *dada* for the first time! West was waving at them from across the park, and out it came."

Lily's hand flew to her heart. "Oh, that's so special! What amazing timing. West is the man of the hour, after all! Good boys."

Max spun three quick circles at the end of his leash and let out a yip, prompting a fit of giggles from the boys.

"I wasn't talking to you, silly. I mean the twins. You're a good boy too, though." Lily gave the dog a quick rub behind his ears before offering Zach and Zane each a high five. "My nephews, the geniuses."

"Oh, good. Here you both are. Say cheese." Haley snapped their photo with her cell phone as she came walking toward them from the tent area.

"Was that for your iPhone photo gallery or the *Chatelaine Daily News*?" Tabitha teased. Haley worked as a freelance journalist, with dreams of becoming a serious investigative reporter. Much to her frustration, thus far, the majority of her earnings came from writing fluff pieces for the local paper.

"Both." Hayley shrugged. "Yes, you're my family and I'm saving this picture because you all look adorable. Love the matching outfits on the boys, by the way. But this event is front-page news and I need some pictures to accompany my article."

Tabitha's gaze darted toward Haley. "Front-page news? Are you serious?"

"Yes, this is Chatelaine, remember? And West is a town hero now—a 'legend.' Word has it that's what the sheriff is going to call him in the speech he's about to give."

Of course Sheriff Cooper was planning on giving a speech. Tabitha wondered if he also intended on mentioning the job offer in his remarks. She wouldn't be surprised.

"So if you're writing this up for the paper, what happened to that top secret project you mentioned a while back?" Lily asked.

"It's still happening, and it's still top secret." Haley mimed locking her lips with a key.

Tabitha looked at Lily and shrugged. So much for finding out what their sister was up to.

"Come on, we don't want to miss the big speech." Haley snapped a few more quick photos before leading the way to the tent, where West stood just to the right of the podium and a beaming Sheriff Cooper.

Tabitha glanced around at the crowd and her heart

warmed. Nearly the entire town had turned out to welcome West home. Lily's husband Asa waved at her from the Cowgirl Café food booth, where he helped his sister Bea Fortune serve customers. Tabitha waved back. She couldn't help but feel a bit overcome by all of the love being heaped on West.

He deserves this. A warm, fuzzy feeling came over her. *No matter what happens between West and me, he's a good man.* Years from now, she could show Zach and Zane the article Haley wrote for the paper and tell the boys all about how their daddy was a town hero. Maybe they'd even remember being there, tucked into their stroller in their matching cotton muslin shortie rompers, printed with whimsical cowboy boots and horseshoes.

Doubtful, but it was a nice thought. In any event, she was glad she'd have the photos to share with them when they got older.

But just as the sheriff tapped the microphone to begin his speech and the cheers of the crown died down, Tabitha caught a snippet of a nearby conversation that put an instant damper on her excitement.

"Bless Tabitha's heart. I can't imagine being in her shoes," someone said in a voice with a syrupy-sweet Texas drawl. "West had to fake his death in order to protect her from that awful man, and she didn't even know he was alive. She thought he was dead this entire time, just like the rest of us. Such a shame. He missed the birth of his twins and everything."

West was back, alive and well, and people were still blessing her heart. Would it *ever* stop?

She shifted from one foot to the other, and tried to concentrate on what Sheriff Cooper was saying, but then another voice chimed in.

"I'm sure that's what Tabitha wants everyone to believe, but I heard something entirely different went down. Rumor around town has it that West freaked out when he found out she was pregnant with twins, so he faked his death instead of dumping her. He just upped and disappeared, leaving her to raise those two little boys on her own."

What?

Tabitha's entire body went cold, despite the warm breeze and the sun shining high in the big Texas sky. Not one word of the gossip was true. Tabitha knew that much for certain. She didn't even know she was pregnant until after West had been "murdered," so there was no way West could've known.

True or not, though, she was awash in humiliation to be the subject of such a degrading rumor. Was this really what people thought of her? Of West?

She blinked hard against the sudden sting of tears as Courtney Riddle's face came to the forefront of her mind. Her comment from playgroup the other day rang in Tabitha's head like a terrible bell.

Bless your heart, Tabitha. Do you have any plans for Mother's Day?

The urge to turn around and see if Courtney was part of the conversation taking place behind her was almost overwhelming. She knew she should rise above the gossip and hold her head high, but what she really wanted to do was march straight over there and give the busybodies, whoever they were, a piece of her mind.

"Don't listen to them," Lily whispered as she took hold of Tabitha's hand. "They're just mean girls, and you know the truth about West. He loves you, and he loves his boys. That's the only thing that matters."

She's right. Tabitha nodded, shot her triplet a watery smile and thanked her lucky stars once again that her biological sisters were back in her life. Then she took hold of Haley's hand, so the three of them were linked together. The Perry sisters—they'd been lost to each other and now they were found again, just like West. She had so much to be thankful for.

But a little bit of the shine had worn off the day all the same, leaving her feeling like she was holding on tight to a piece of the fool's gold that was still buried beneath the very ground on which she stood.

Chapter Seven

West had never shaken so many hands in his life.

Once the sheriff had finished his effusive speech, he tried to make his way back to Tabitha and the twins, but he couldn't take a step without someone wanting to shower him with well-wishes. It was nice, but also humbling. He didn't deserve a ticker-tape parade. The man he'd been before and the decisions he'd made hadn't always been honorable. Life was more complicated than that. This was his second chance in more ways than one, and he didn't want to screw it up.

"Howdy, brother." Camden grinned as West finished shaking yet another hand. Then, once they were alone—relatively speaking, of course—he gave him a one-armed hug and handed him a red Solo cup. "Try this. It's homemade root beer from Bea's new place, the Cowgirl Café."

West took a sip. It was frothy and sweet, with hints of vanilla and sugar cane, and it might have been the best thing he'd ever tasted. "This is delicious."

"Right?" Camden nodded toward the café's booth, just to the left of the tent, where a line of people stretched all the way to a cluster of picnic tables covered in red-checkered cloths. "I just saved you at least a half hour of standing in line. Although, since you're the town hero and all you could probably cut straight to the front."

"Stop," West said, frowning into his root beer. He didn't feel like a hero. Heroes didn't typically leave a brokenhearted woman and two fatherless babies in their wake. "Have you seen Tabitha? I keep trying to make my way toward her, but now I don't see her anywhere."

"She's around here somewhere with Lily and Haley." Camden's gaze swept the crowd, and he shrugged. "Don't worry. We'll find her. Real quick, though. Is the rumor I'm hearing true?"

"Rumor?" West tensed. "What rumor?"

"According to the Chatelaine grapevine, you're going back to work as the county prosecutor."

West shook his head. "Nope. Not true—at least not yet. Sheriff Cooper made me an offer, and I told him I need to think about it. I loved the job—you know that—but in retrospect, I'm not sure it's the best thing now that I have a family. And I guess I've also come to realize there's more to life than work."

"Totally understandable. And you know there's a job for you at the ranch if you want to keep your cowboy hat on. I was serious the other day when I mentioned it. I could use some help getting the legalities and insurance paperwork straightened out for the equestrian school. It's all a lot more than I'd anticipated. Even part-time help from Chatelaine's most capable attorney would be appreciated." Camden sighed.

"I'll keep that in mind. I've got a lot to think about, but know that you can always come to me if you're feeling overwhelmed, brother." *Family first*, West thought. From now on, that was his new motto. It would just take a little getting used to, that's all.

"Thanks, man." Camden's eyes lit up as his gaze landed on someone just over West's shoulder. "Hey, look. I told you we'd find her."

West turned to find Tabitha pushing the twins' stroller toward them. Zach and Zane were both fast asleep with their little blond heads nestled together.

"Hi, Tabitha. Good to see you." Camden gave Tabitha a hug and pointed his cup toward the stroller. "Look at my nephews. They're adorable, even when they're unconscious."

"I think they're worn out from all the excitement." Tabitha laughed, but her smile didn't quite reach her eyes. "Actually, I have big news for the town hero here."

She gave West a gentle shoulder bump. "The twins called you dada earlier when they were waving at you."

"They did?" Now *that* was something really worth celebrating. Joy filled West like sunshine.

"They sure did." She grinned up at him, but something still felt off.

He wondered if she'd ever really let him back in, or had he missed his chance for good? West had never allowed himself to think that way since his return, but lately the thought had begun to burrow its way into his consciousness. Like a burr in a horse's mane that ended up working its way under the saddle pad and causing all sorts of trouble.

"That's the best news I've heard all day," West said, and he meant it. He squatted so he was on eye level with his sons and wished they'd wake up and say it again.

But they were far off in dreamland, a world away from Chatelaine Park and the homecoming that still felt somewhat like trying to fit a square peg into a round hole. And West was more aware than ever that *he* was the square peg. He was the problem that still needed fixing.

"I think we should have a birthday party for the boys." He stood and fixed his gaze with Tabitha's. "What do you think?"

Her eyes widened in surprise. "Oh, sure. I'm sure Zach and Zane would love that."

"Great. It's a date, then." West nodded, but there was still one detail to figure out. "When exactly is their birthday, though?"

Camden's eyebrows rose before he could hide his surprise at the question. Then he quickly dropped his gaze toward the concrete floor of the park pavilion.

"It's the thirtieth," Tabitha said with a nod, completely unfazed, and West realized she hadn't expected him to know the date.

Fair, given the circumstances, but he still felt like an imposter dad asking the question. When West had been in third grade, his father had forgotten his birthday, prompting another explosive fight between his parents. Like father, like son?

No.

West's jaw clenched.

Not if he could help it.

"The thirtieth," he echoed, and then he wrapped an arm around Tabitha's shoulders and pretended not to notice the way history kept worming its way between them.

For better or for worse.

Tabitha couldn't stop thinking about the gossip she'd overheard at the picnic. Three days had passed since the celebration, and she still hadn't mentioned it to West. What was the point? At first, she'd kept quiet because she hadn't wanted to ruin the day for him. Whether or not the sheriff's intentions were a bit self-serving didn't really matter. She wanted West to remember being honored by the town, not being bad-mouthed behind his back.

Afterward, she still couldn't bring it up because, much to her astonishment, the day after the picnic, he'd signed up for an online course in rearing twins. While she worked on her web development business, West either spent his time with Zach and Zane or put together elaborate organizational spreadsheets for everything from meal planning to bath times. More than once, when she'd stolen a free moment to zip into the kitchen to pre-pack a few lunches for the boys, she'd found the task had already been done. Now when she opened her refrigerator, color-coded containers were all lined up in a neat row—blue for breakfast, red for snacks, yellow for lunch and green for dinner. He was trying so hard. She didn't have the heart to tell him that someone had been saying such awful things about the two of them. As the days wore on, it seemed less and less important, even to Tabitha.

Late Tuesday afternoon, she managed to finish a site design for one of her top clients a full week before her deadline. After months of barely keeping up, it felt like a full-blown miracle.

West was busy with more meal planning while the boys sat in their matching highchairs munching on peas and carrots.

"Do you want to share a pizza tonight after the boys finish their dinner? And maybe a glass of wine?" she asked as she closed her laptop.

West popped the lid on a green Tupperware container, looked up and grinned at her. "That sounds perfect. If I eat another well-balanced meal, I might not know what to do with myself." He shot a wink at one of the babies. "No offense, Zach. I know how much you love your veggies."

"West." Tabitha bit back a smile. "That's Zane."

"Of course it is." West sighed, but he didn't tense up the way he usually did when he mixed up the twins. It was nice to see him developing a little confidence in the daddy department—yet another reason not to mention nasty town gossip.

Tabitha joined him in the kitchen and once plates were cleared and chins wiped, the boys sat on their blanket in the living room with a stack of chunky puzzles. The doorbell rang as West helped Zach fit a zebra puzzle piece in place.

"Oh, great. The pizza is already here." Tabitha

handed Zane a monkey puzzle piece and pointed to the spot where it went. "I'm famished."

"I'll get it." West stood and ruffled Zach's hair. "Be right back, munchkin."

He jogged to the front door in his sock feet, but instead of opening it, he turned back to face Tabitha after he'd glanced through the peephole.

"What is it?" Tabitha asked.

"Well, it's definitely not the pizza." West arched an eyebrow. "It's Freya Fortune."

"Again?" Another impromptu visit from West's newly discovered step-grandmother? Things were beginning to seem a little strange in that department.

"This is weird, isn't it?" West mused, raking a hand through his hair.

"Not as weird as us leaving her standing on the porch for several long minutes." The older woman was probably just lonely. There were a lot of Fortunes, after all. It might take her a while to figure out where she fit. "Go ahead and let her in."

West nodded and swung the door open. "Freya, what a surprise."

"I hope you don't mind that I popped by again. I promise it's not going to become a habit." Freya held up a giant shopping bag from GreatStore. "I just wanted to bring by a few gifts for the twins."

"Oh, that's lovely, Freya." Tabitha beckoned her inside while West held the door open for her and relieved her of the burden of the overstuffed shopping bag.

"Something tells me you might have gone overboard," he said, pretending to struggle to pick up the bag.

"Oh, stop." Freya laughed and gave him a playful swat. "You know it's a grandparent's job to spoil the little ones. That goes double for great-grandparents. And, look! There they are. Zach and Zane, aren't you two just too precious for words?"

West ushered Freya inside, and after letting the twins rip open their packages, the adults sat on the sofa to watch the boys explore their new toys on their play blanket.

"Thank you again, Freya. This was really sweet, but West was right. You definitely went overboard. Promise me you're going to come empty-handed to the boys' birthday party later this month," Tabitha said.

"We'll see about that." Freya winked. "I'm not making any promises."

Zach picked up a plastic mallet and banged away on a colorful xylophone while Zane clapped along with the uneven beat.

"They really are the sweetest children. Although, if I'm being totally honest, the gifts weren't the only reason I wanted to come by." Freya shot West and Tabitha an apologetic glance.

"You don't need an excuse to visit the boys. You're welcome here anytime," Tabitha said. The surprise visits were admittedly a little odd, but she didn't want the older woman to think she had to back up a dump truck full of toys to the front door every time she wanted to come over.

West leaned forward on the sofa, narrowing his gaze slightly at Freya seated across from them. Tabitha could practically hear his brain click into lawyer mode.

There was still so much about her they didn't know. Which meant there was no doubt in Tabitha's mind that West would want to find out more about this stranger who'd recently turned up in everyone's lives. "Was there another reason in particular that you wanted to see us?"

"Yes, there is." Freya cleared her throat as she gazed wistfully at the twins. "Last time I was here, I mentioned I had a daughter and we'd become estranged."

"I'm so sorry about that, Freya. That must be really hard," Tabitha said. She couldn't imagine being separated from either one of the twins for any reason—not even when they were older and all grown up. It would have felt like losing a big chunk of her heart.

What must have happened to cause such ill will between Freya and her daughter?

"It is." The older woman's eyes grew misty. "I guess I'm just feeling a little vulnerable and exposed after sharing such difficult and personal information with the two of you. I don't talk very often about the estrangement. In fact, I can't remember the last time I told anyone about my daughter. I haven't seen Renee in many years."

"As you know, the Fortune family is well acquainted with estrangement, so we can sympathize," West said.

We. As if they were a couple...a *family.* Tabitha waited for the inevitable wave of anxiety to wash over her at the idea, but it never came. Not this time.

"Maybe you should try reaching out to her. Time has a way of healing old wounds." Tabitha stole a glance at West. Over a year and a half had passed since she'd ended their engagement. Thinking about their breakup was feeling less and less like pressing a tender bruise, especially now that he'd come home.

"I don't even know where Renee is. I haven't spoken to her in decades." Freya shook her head, her hand fluttering to the silk bow at the collar of her blouse like a nervous bird.

Decades?

Tabitha was at a loss for words. A mother and child, separated for twenty or thirty years... She couldn't fathom anything sadder.

"Have you ever tried to find her?" West asked.

She nodded. "Several times throughout the years, but I haven't had any luck."

Tabitha's chest felt heavy all of a sudden. "I'm so sorry, Freya. You must be heartbroken."

"We're glad you opened up to us about this." West reached for the woman's hand and wove his fingers through hers. "If you ever need anyone to talk to about Renee, we're always here for you."

Longing whispered through Tabitha as West caressed the back of Freya's hand with slow, tender circles of the pad of his thumb. Regret tugged at her heart. All over the world, there were people like Freya, separated from their loved ones for all sorts of reasons. Tabitha was one of the lucky ones. She'd been miraculously reunited with her sisters, and after so many months of missing West and wishing she could see him again, yearning for him to know his children and be part of their lives, her wildest dreams had been granted. He was back, and he was sitting right beside her, giving her every indication that he wanted to start over.

And still Tabitha was afraid to open her heart and let him all the way in. Maybe she needed this heart-to-heart even more than Freya did.

She offered West's step-granny her sincerest smile. "One more thing, Freya. Don't ever give up. Trust me on this—life has a way of surprising you when you least expect it. Prayers are answered every day, and dreams really do come true."

Was it really so hard to take the biggest leap of all and believe in a happy-ever-after?

Chapter Eight

The next day, Tabitha decided she couldn't keep postponing the inevitable, and she did the one thing she'd been dreading since West's return to Chatelaine. She called her adoptive parents.

She'd put it off far too long already. Thus far, she'd managed to limit recent communication with the Buckinghams to text messages and emails. In any other family unit, that probably would've seemed strange. Her former fiancé had come back from the dead, after all. If news like that didn't warrant a phone call, what did?

But her parents had never been warm or fuzzy. Tabitha couldn't remember the last time that Lyle or Grace, or her adoptive brother Alec, had called her out of the blue. Why spend aimless minutes chitchatting when you could shoot off a text instead?

"Tabitha?" Her mom sounded confused when she answered the Buckingham landline, as if she'd briefly forgotten she had a daughter.

Tabitha knew better than to take it personally. What else should she expect from the couple who'd adopted her purely because her blond hair and blue eyes matched the toddler Grace had given birth to a few years prior? Lily and Haley had been raised in foster care after their parents' accident, while Tabitha had drawn the lucky straw. She'd grown up in a mini mansion, she'd gone to all the best schools, and she'd been showered with every material thing a little girl could ever want, including a pony. But she and Alec had also spent more time with their nanny than they had with their parents, all the way through high school.

Still, things could've been so much worse. She was the *lucky* Perry triplet. Tabitha never knew whether to feel guilty or grateful about her good fortune. Most of the time, thinking about it just made her sad.

"Hi, Mom. Happy Mother's Day," Tabitha said.

"Mother's Day is still a few days away," Grace Buckingham said, sounding even more baffled.

Tabitha should've stuck to texting.

"I know, but you mentioned that you and Dad have that golf tournament on Sunday, so I won't get to see you on the actual day." It was a relief, honestly. Tabitha wanted to spend a quiet day with her boys instead of trying to make two babies behave at the Buckinghams' country club, where they always insisted on going for special occasions.

"Well, thank you, then. And thank you for the article you sent over from the *Chatelaine Daily News*. It looks like West is going to have his old job back in no time."

And there it was—the other reason Tabitha had been reluctant to speak to her parents. If Sheriff Cooper was the president of the West Fortune fan club, then Lyle and Grace Buckingham were surely co-VPs.

Not that they'd spent much time with him. They hadn't had to. His law degree and last name said it all.

Tabitha bristled. "That's not what the article said, Mom."

"Honey, it sounds like you need to learn how to read between the lines. The sheriff threw the man a party and the entire town came. The handwriting is on the wall. You should be thrilled."

So, so thrilled. Tabitha squeezed her eyes closed tight. Of all the things that had originally made her fall in love with West, his job and legendary Texas family ranked dead last on the list. Tabitha had fallen in love with West's earnestness. His integrity. And the way he cared so much about others. It wasn't the trappings of his legal career that drew her to him, but rather the way he believed so strongly in protecting the innocent.

Look where that got us, she thought with a bitter-sweet clench of her heart.

"West hasn't made any decisions about his future yet," she said in as firm as a voice as she could muster.

"Surely that doesn't include the wedding. The twins are about to turn one year old, Tabitha. It's high time their parents get married. Please tell me you've set a date," her mother said. Because goodness gracious, what must her country club friends think?

"West has only been home for a week. Give us time." Tabitha took a deep breath. She knew she should've told her family she'd broken off the engagement, but once West had been declared legally dead, she just didn't have it in her to relive that awful fight. Especially not with the Buckinghams. "Things are complicated."

Grace huffed out a breath. "I don't see why they should be. He's living with you, isn't he?"

"For the boys. West needs to get to know his sons." She needed to switch gears and fast. There'd been a reason for her call, and it was *not* to discuss dates for a hypothetical wedding that technically no longer existed. If she didn't put an end to the West talk, her mother would start tossing out ideas for venues and wedding planners and caterers, just like she'd done before. *Only the best for the Buckinghams!* It was the family motto, after all. "Would you like to have lunch tomorrow? As an early Mother's Day celebration since you and Daddy have plans on Sunday?"

"Oh." Grace paused for a beat. Clearly the idea of making alternate plans so she could actually see her daughter for Mother's Day had never crossed her mind. "That sounds nice. We can meet at the club."

Tabitha much preferred the Cowgirl Café in Chatelaine or, if she insisted on someplace fancy, the Chatelaine Bar and Grill. But, of course, her mother would expect her to schlep all the way to Houston with the twins so they could see and be seen at the posh country club.

She really shouldn't complain, though. The drive wasn't bad. The boys liked looking at the cattle and hay bales through the car windows on the way. And this was supposed to be a Mother's Day celebration.

"Super. I'm looking forward to it, Mom. I'm sure the twins will be happy to see you."

"Perfect. I'll make an eleven a.m. reservation for six." Grace's voice was already drifting off, even though the call hadn't technically ended.

"Wait!" Tabitha blurted. "Six? But it's just you, me and the boys."

"Don't be silly, honey. Your daddy will want to be there. And we haven't seen West in years. He'll be there too, obviously."

Obviously.

Tabitha bit her lip and tried to think of any and every reasonable excuse for West to stay back in Chatelaine. But within seconds, it was too late. A click followed by a dial tone sounded from the other end. Her mother had already hung up the phone.

Grace Buckingham had spoken.

West removed his Stetson with one hand and kept hold of Zane's car seat with the other as he and Tabitha entered the Buckinghams' country club. Tabitha held Zach's car seat and seemed to stiffen a little the moment they crossed the threshold of the stately building. West understood. With its huge white-columned exterior and marble tiled entrance, the River Oaks Country Club felt like it was a world away from Chatelaine. A different planet, even. Try as he might, he could never picture Tabitha growing up in a place like this.

She had, though. She'd done it all—tennis lessons, horseback riding, all the rich girl hobbies. And the moment she'd been old enough to choose a life for herself, she'd hotfooted it back to Chatelaine, where her birth parents were from. She'd been determined to build her own life there, and she'd done just that, without the Buckinghams' help. It was one of the things West admired most about her. Her resilience, her love for her roots, her fiercely independent streak...even if he was still having trouble getting fully back in her good graces due to that hard-fought independence of hers.

"Thanks for this," Tabitha said as she blew out a big breath. "I don't know what I was thinking. I should've just told my parents the truth instead of asking you to pretend we were still engaged."

"It's one meal. I think I can handle it." He shot her a reassuring wink. West knew he probably shouldn't read anything into the fact that she was so hesitant to tell the Buckinghams the truth, but he couldn't help seeing it as a tiny spark of hope. If she wanted to act like they were still a real couple, he was all for it.

"I'm a terrible liar. They're going to know we're faking it."

"No, they won't," West countered, because *he* wouldn't be faking anything. He still loved Tabitha with his whole heart. "Trust me."

Her lips quirked into a smile. "You seem awfully sure of yourself, cowboy."

"Always." He blew her a kiss.

Tabitha's face went as pink as the bouquet of fresh peonies that stood on a polished oak table in the center of the country club lobby. Then she spotted her father bustling toward them from the dining room and relaxed as she assumed the air kiss had been for his benefit.

It hadn't.

"West, Tabitha. Here you are!" Lyle Buckingham gave West a hearty slap on the back. "So good to see you, son. You gave us a real scare, you know."

"I'm sorry, sir. It couldn't be helped."

"Of course it couldn't. You did what you had to do. *Heroic*—that's what it was." Lyle bent down to give Tabitha a kiss on the cheek. "I hope you know that most men wouldn't have made the kind of sacrifice that West made for you."

"Um." Tabitha's blush deepened at least three shades as she held up her left hand and wiggled her fingers to show off her engagement ring. "You're absolutely right. He's a keeper."

West wrapped his free arm around Tabitha and gave her shoulder a squeeze. *We've got this.* "Shall we get seated, Lyle? We don't want to keep Grace waiting."

"Certainly. Then we can dote on our grandbabies for a bit. Right this way." Lyle took Zach's car seat from Tabitha and led them down a hallway with plush red carpet toward the dining room.

Grace Buckingham sat at a table for six in a prime location, overlooking the club's vast, emerald-green golf course. When she spotted their group approaching, she waved but didn't get up.

They spent several long moments exchanging greetings and getting the twins situated in their highchairs, and then Tabitha handed her mother a clear floral box containing a single purple orchid.

"Happy early Mother's Day, Mom," she said.

"Thank you, honey." Grace cast the flower a curious glance. "But what is this, exactly?"

"It's a wrist corsage. Just a sweet Southern tradition that I'd forgotten about. You know how I love flowers, so I thought it might be fun to make it a new Mother's Day family tradition of our own." Tabitha opened the box and gently plucked the orchid from inside. "I got purple because I knew it was your favorite color. I can help you put it on."

She held the flower toward her mother.

Grace held up a hand. "Oh, I don't think so. Not now. That's a little gauche for our surroundings, don't you think?"

Tabitha's face fell, and West had a very sudden, very real urge to sweep her and the boys off and disappear again. They could all vanish together this time.

"It's very thoughtful, though. Thank you." Grace replaced the orchid in the box and tucked it away in her handbag, where it would probably never see the light of day again. "So, when is the wedding?"

Nothing like cutting straight to the chase.

"I already told you, Mom. We haven't decided yet." Tabitha unfolded her napkin and placed it in her lap. "West has only been back a week."

"Well, honey." Grace cast a pointed look at the twins. "Don't you think you two need to make this official sooner rather than later?"

As if two one-year-olds cared a whit about their parents' marital status.

"Don't worry, ma'am. The boys couldn't be happier. They're little love sponges. Tabitha has done a phenomenal job raising them," West said, perhaps a little too sharply. But he wasn't going to sit there and let anyone imply that the life she'd created—the one that filled her with so much joy—was anything less than perfect. "That being said, I'd marry your daughter right this minute if I could."

Tabitha let out a strangled laugh.

He arched a brow at her and reached for her hand under the table, giving it a squeeze, so she'd know he was telling the complete and utter truth.

"If we're going to have it here at the country club, we need to reserve a date as soon as possible. I checked with the staff and they're booking eighteen months out, if you can believe that. *Eighteen months.*" Grace sat up a little more primly. "Not to worry. I pulled some strings, and I think we can sneak you in much sooner. There are only two dates this summer to choose from so we should probably do it now."

Tabitha shook her head. "We've already talked about this. West and I want to get married in Chatelaine, remember?"

Lyle and Grace exchanged a glance.

"But honey, that was before," Lyle said with exaggerated patience, as if talking to a child.

West thought he might need to hide Tabitha's steak knife. Possibly her fork, as well.

"Before what, exactly?" Tabitha asked in clipped syllables.

"Before your fiancé came back from the dead." Grace sighed. "Honestly, Tabitha. West was already

a Fortune and the county prosecutor. Now he's a genuine Texas *legend*. He's going to go down in history.
Your darling boys might even read about him in their
schoolbooks someday."

"West Fortune can't get married at that tiny church
in Chatelaine," Lyle said with a shake of his head.

Now West might need to hide his own cutlery. This
was getting out of hand.

"West Fortune is going to marry Tabitha Buckingham wherever her heart desires," he said flatly. He met
both of her parents' gazes and held direct eye contact
until they each looked away, focusing instead on the
crisp table linens or the ridiculously opulent crystal
water goblets. "Understood?"

Grace sniffed. "Of course, it's *your* wedding. We
just want the very best for the two of you, that's all."

"Mom, the best doesn't always mean the most expensive or the fanciest. To me, the best means the
most meaningful. The most special. And what's really going to make our wedding special is the two of
us. Our boys. Our *home*…and that's in Chatelaine,
not here." Tabitha face lit up as she talked about their
wedding. It was almost as if she thought it might really happen someday.

Which West wanted more than anything in the
world.

When neither one of her parents said anything in
response, she pushed her chair back and placed her
napkin in her empty seat. "If everyone will excuse
me, I need to go to the ladies' room."

"That's fine, honey. We'll keep an eye on the boys.

We brought them each a little present." Grace reached into her bag to remove two small packages wrapped in matching baby-blue paper. As she did so, the corsage box tumbled to the floor.

Grace didn't notice, but Tabitha did. The purple orchid sat there on the floor, forgotten. She left the table without another word.

"Mama?" Zach's tiny forehead puckered.

Beside him, Zane swiveled in his highchair, looking for Tabitha.

"Mama will be right back, kiddos. I promise," West said.

Grace set the wrapped gifts on their respective highchair trays and the boys immediately tore into the wrapping paper, happily distracted from their mother's absence.

"I'll be right back, as well." West pushed back from the table before anyone could protest.

As expected, Tabitha hadn't needed to visit the ladies' room. He found her in a cozy nook just off the entrance to the dining room, sitting on a velvet settee surrounded by bookshelves. She gave a little start when he made his way around the corner shelf and sat down beside her.

"You're here," she said quietly.

And I always will be. "I wanted to make sure you were okay. That was a little intense back there."

"But how did you know where to find me? This place is huge." She gestured to the country club's high ceilings and green toile wallpaper. Just around the corner, a grand, curved staircase swept into view.

"You told me about this little nook on our very first date." The memory filled West's chest with warmth. "You said your mom and dad loved to spend time at their club when you were a little girl, but you never liked it here. So you'd sneak off to a hidden reading nook by the dining room and hide until someone came and found you. You said it was always your brother Alec."

"It was always Alec." She nodded, eyes shining bright. "I can't believe you remember that story. Our first date was years ago."

"I remember everything, sweetheart. And I clung to those memories while I was in hiding. They're what kept me going. All I wanted was to get back home." He swallowed, trying his best not to say everything that was in his heart. It wouldn't be fair. She wasn't ready to hear it yet…but he just couldn't keep it inside anymore. "All I wanted was to get back home to *you* and tell you how sorry I was for breaking your heart. I'd have given you the world for another chance. All the babies your heart desired."

"Maybe you were just lonely and missing home," she said, her voice cracking ever so slightly.

"I know exactly who I was missing, babe." He lifted her hand and pressed a tender kiss to her knuckles.

She smiled at him and then cupped his face in her hands and kissed him as gently as if he might break. No, as if *they* might break…as if one wrong move or word might tear apart the new, fragile connection they'd been building. She didn't rush like last time, when they'd been in such a hurry to come together.

They'd been chasing a memory then, but this wasn't yesterday's kiss. It belonged to this moment and this moment only.

Her lips were warm and honey-sweet, because Tabitha had always been every bit as beautiful on the inside as she was on the outside. She represented everything West had always wanted when he was a kid. Kindness, goodness, stability. *Love.* Maybe that's why he'd run scared before. He couldn't imagine a dream like that ever being real. Surely he'd screw it up somehow.

But West had done enough running for one lifetime. His boots weren't budging. Not anymore.

"Why are my parents like that?" she murmured when she pulled away, eyes shining bright with unshed tears. "I never felt like I fit in here, and every time I come back, it's always the same. I'm nothing like them."

"You're not, and that's okay, because the person you are is beautiful. No matter what anyone says or how they make you feel. You're perfect just the way you are, Tabs."

"I like that you think so, even if it's not true." She let out a quiet laugh. "I'm hardly perfect. Case in point—I roped you into this lunch so we could lie to my family."

A grin tugged at the corner of his mouth. "I think we nailed it."

"Seriously, West. Thank you for this. You were amazing in there." Her gaze went soft, like she was looking at him through rose-colored glasses. It had been a long time since Tabitha had looked at him like that, and that one look meant more to him than all the hero talk in the world.

Hers was the only opinion that mattered.

"Anything for you, darlin'."

Chapter Nine

After the disastrous lunch at the country club with the Buckinghams, Tabitha forgot all about Mother's Day. In her mind, the holiday was over and done with. She'd tried her best to celebrate her mom and, as per usual, Tabitha and Grace weren't on the same page. They were hardly even in the same *book*, for that matter.

Funnily enough, the things West had said to her while they'd been tucked away in the reading nook had truly made her feel better. She didn't fit in with her adoptive family, but she definitely belonged in Chatelaine. The moment they'd crossed the town border on their way back home, she'd finally been able to breathe a little easier. There was no way on God's green earth they were getting married at her parents' country club.

You're not getting married at all, *remember?*

Tabitha toyed with her engagement ring, which was once again sparkling on her ring finger. She'd placed it there before lunch with the Buckinghams for obvious reasons, and three days later, it was still there, shining like a star in the sweeping Texas sky.

Tabitha really needed to get a grip. She and West still weren't together as a couple. After they'd come home from the day trip to Houston, they'd slipped right back into their co-parenting routine as if the kiss in the reading nook had never happened. Tabitha wasn't sure what to make of it. A part of her thought that West was simply honoring her request for time and space, which should have been a relief. It was what she wanted, after all.

But another part of her knew the truth, and that truth was becoming harder and harder to ignore: her resistance was crumbling.

Their kiss the other day had been nothing like the night they'd spent together. She hadn't been kissing the man who she'd loved and lost. When she pressed her lips to his at the country club, she'd been kissing the new West Fortune. She'd been kissing the man who'd rocked their babies to sleep at night, who'd thrown himself into fatherhood with every last bit of his heart, who'd been putting her needs first for a change and had still yet to commit himself to returning to work at the prosecutor's office.

It couldn't last, though, could it? This little slice of heaven was only temporary. Things would have to change, eventually. West had wanted to devote precious days to getting to know his children, but they couldn't stop time forever. Their world would start spinning again soon, and Tabitha didn't know what would become of these new, overwhelming feelings that were blossoming in the most secret parts of her heart.

So she did her best to mirror West's behavior and threw herself into parenthood. They ate together, cooked together, cared for the boys together…and then at night, they went their separate ways. West on the sofa in the living room and Tabitha alone in her bed, where she sometimes dreamed that this simple time could stretch clear on into the horizon, where the setting sun always made the wide-open spaces of rural Texas look like liquid gold. Precious and priceless, like the fantasy that the miners had been chasing all those years ago. The only thing she'd change would be the sleeping arrangements. She ached for West every single night.

Pretending they were still engaged had apparently gone straight to her head.

Tabitha swallowed as she folded a pile of freshly washed onesies in the nursery. She needed to stop letting her feelings get to her and remember why she and West were living under the same roof. He was here for the twins, not her.

"Knock, knock." West rapped his knuckles softly on the half-closed door and poked his head inside the room. The boys were still fast asleep, lying on their tummies in matching poses. Identical twins to their very core. "What's going on in here? It's barely the crack of dawn."

"Just doing a few chores before the babies wake up and the day descends into chaos," she whispered.

"On Mother's Day?" West gave her a stern look and shook his head. "I don't think so. C'mere."

He gestured to her with a beckoning finger. How could Tabitha say no? He was barely awake, with charmingly rumpled bedhead, and he'd still managed to remember it was Mother's Day, whereas the date on the calendar had completely slipped her mind. She'd woken up with the sun and moved quietly about the house while everyone kept sleeping.

Tabitha actually loved being the first one up. It warmed her heart knowing that the people she treasured most in this world were all safe, sleeping peacefully under the same roof. It was such a simple little thing to take pleasure in. But once upon a time, it had seemed like a pipe dream. How things had changed.

She placed the folded onesie on top of the pile and slipped out of the nursery, following West through the dimly lit hall until they were in the living room.

Tabitha blinked. Everything looked different than it had the night before. Yellow-and-white streamers hung from the ceiling and a banner that said Happy Mother's Day was draped from one end of the big picture window to the other. A silver ice bucket sat on the kitchen counter with a foil-wrapped bottle propped inside, right next to a pitcher of what looked like freshly squeezed, pulpy orange juice and four thin champagne flutes.

"When did you do all of this?" She swiveled her gaze back to West, who seemed to be hiding something behind his back.

He shrugged one shoulder, and the plain white tee he always slept in stretched nicely across his chest. "Mostly last night after you went to bed. I wanted to surprise you. Happy Mother's Day, Tabs."

All her breath seemed to bottle up tight in her chest as he produced a small florist's box from behind his back—clear plastic, with a corsage made of four buttery yellow roses nestled inside. The flowers were trimmed with white lace and attached to a bracelet of faux pearls.

"Oh, West." Blinking back tears, Tabitha pressed her fingertips to her lips. It was undoubtedly the most beautiful wrist corsage she'd ever seen.

West gave her a crooked grin, and what he said next made it all the more special. "For my yellow rose of Texas. There are four rosebuds there, one for each of us—you, me and the twins. I'm sorry I wasn't here to celebrate last year, but we can make this our own family tradition, starting right now. What do you say?"

Tabitha's heart hammered against her rib cage. He'd really been paying attention at lunch, hadn't he? Her efforts to start a tradition with her mom hadn't panned out, so he'd put that shattered dream back together and made it their own.

"I love it," she whispered, and this time she wasn't simply trying to be quiet because the twins were still sleeping. Her throat was clogged with emotion and all the things she suddenly wanted to say…things she knew might get her in trouble.

"Here, let me." West opened the box, releasing the sweet perfume of the roses into the air. Tabitha's head spun. "Give me your hand."

She let out a soft laugh. "Now? I'm in my nightgown."

"They'll complement each other beautifully." He winked as he took her hand and gently slid the flowers in place on her wrist.

She turned her hand to and fro, marveling at the tiny arrangement and all that those four roses symbolized. Not just a tradition, but a promise. A future, all wrapped up in soft yellow petals and lace. "I can't believe you did this."

"Just wait. There's more," he said.

Tabitha's forehead scrunched and she glanced around, searching for his meaning. That's when the number of champagne flutes on the counter finally struck her as odd. "Four glasses? Are we expecting company?"

Right on cue, the doorbell rang.

"Surprise!" Haley and Lily gushed in unison when Tabitha opened the door.

Her sisters were both still dressed in their pajamas— Haley in demure polka dots and Lily's decorated with tumbling puppy dogs who seemed to bear a striking resemblance to Max. Haley carried a cake stand with a beautifully frosted yellow cake sitting atop it, and Lily had an armful of gift bags.

Tabitha shook her head. "What's going on here? It's not even seven o'clock in the morning."

"Hence our attire," Haley said with an arch of her eyebrows.

"It's a surprise Mother's Day pajama party." Lily flashed West a grin over Tabitha's shoulder. "It was West's idea. He wanted to surprise you."

Haley's eyes sparkled. "Did it work? Are you surprised?"

"Surprised would be an understatement." Tabitha

laughed and held the door open wide. "Come on in. Please. The boys aren't even up yet."

"Oh, that was intentional. You're not lifting a finger this morning, hon. Zach and Zane's aunties are here, and we're getting the boys up and dressed and fed and all that jazz while you put your feet up and enjoy some cake for breakfast." Haley set the cake plate down next to the ice bucket on the kitchen counter. "Did I mention the cake is mimosa flavored? Orange layer cake with silky champagne cream. Lily made it from scratch."

Tabitha gasped. "You're kidding. I don't remember the GreatStore café serving anything that fancy back when you worked there, Lily."

"That's because this cake is special, just for you." Her sister pulled a face. "But this is my first time trying the recipe, so no promises."

Tabitha took a big inhale. "It smells fantastic. I'm sure it will be amazing."

"Who wants mimosas? I'm ready to pour," West said as he plucked the champagne bottle from the ice bucket.

Haley and Lily both raised their hands.

"Me too, most definitely," Tabitha said.

"That's a given. You get the first glass." West handed her a champagne flute.

She took it but hesitated before taking a sip. "I'm pretty sure I hear the boys stirring in their room."

"No worries. That's our department today." Haley bustled toward the nursery with Lily hot on her heels.

"Try and save us some cake and bubbly, though," Lily shot over her shoulder.

"As if we could consume all of this by ourselves." Tabitha laughed.

Her quiet morning was suddenly filled with the sounds of babbling babies and celebration and more joy than she'd ever thought possible to fit into her modest little cottage. It was such a stark contrast to Mother's Day last year, when she'd been nine months pregnant with swollen ankles and practically on bed rest as she prepared to give birth to twins. As exciting as that time had been, it had also been bittersweet. A day hadn't passed when Tabitha hadn't mourned West. Not just for herself, but for her children. She'd thought they would never know their daddy...had been convinced she was all they'd ever have. Just her and the memories of the man who'd never even known they existed.

And now here they all were, together. Everything she'd been too afraid to hope for, to *pray* for, had somehow still come true. It was almost too much to believe.

Tabitha opened the gifts from her sisters—a scented candle that smelled like the Southern Magnolia trees that grew in Chatelaine, a box of the fudge she loved so much from the gift shop at the mine, a cozy sweatshirt that said *Twin Mom, Doubly Blessed* on the front. Nothing fancy or over-the-top like the gifts the Buckinghams always heaped upon her at Christmas or her birthday. Just little things that showed how well her sisters knew her.

"This is too much, y'all," she said with a catch in her voice.

"It's your very first Mother's Day as a mama," Haley countered, snuggling Zane against her chest. The boys loved cuddling with their aunties. While Zane was happily tucked into Haley's arms, Zach played with a lock of Lily's dark hair.

"And we all wanted to celebrate you." Lily handed Tabitha a small gift bag with a profusion of tissue paper peeking out of the top. "And we saved the best one for last. Go ahead, open it."

The gift bag was lighter than air. Tabitha removed clump after clump of tissue paper, prompting giggles from the twins, who seemed to think it was a game— especially once West wadded the paper into balls and started juggling, putting on a little show for them.

Finally, Tabitha managed to unearth a small silver picture frame at the bottom of the bag. She reached inside for it, certain it must be one of the pictures that Haley had snapped at the picnic in the park the other day. But no…

This photo was older. The image, grainy. But Tabitha knew all four faces by heart.

"Is this…" Her throat closed up before she could finish.

"It's us," Lily said with a wobble in her voice. "When we were babies. And look, there's our mother."

Tears formed in Tabitha's eyes as she scanned the photo, hungry for details. Being adopted by the Buckinghams, Tabitha didn't have a single possession from her infancy. She no longer even had the Perry name. The only way she even recognized the woman pushing the baby stroller in the photo as her mother, Laura, was from newspaper photographs that had appeared in the *Chatelaine Daily News* after the car accident that claimed her parents' lives. When Tabitha first moved to Chatelaine, she'd researched everything she could about her mother and father. The paper had printed old high school graduation photos of her parents, and until now, they were the only faces she'd had to put to their names.

"I can't believe this. Look how beautiful she is." Tabitha ran a trembling fingertip along the outline of her mother's face, round like Haley's. But she had Lily's freckles, and looking at the sparkle in the woman's kind eyes was like peering straight into a mirror. They'd each inherited a part of their mother and still carried her memory with them, wherever they went, for all the world to see.

The sisters were just babies in the photograph, sitting side by side in a wide, triple stroller. Lily was in the middle, flanked by Haley on the left and Tabitha on the right. She could recognize them easily, even as infants.

"Where did you get this?" Tabitha pressed the picture to her heart. What a treasure, and to receive it on her very first Mother's Day was a gift beyond anything she could've imagined.

"Val Hansen found it in some old boxes she'd been going through after selling us the ranch, so she gave it to me. There was so much going on with Asa at the time—our marriage, and realizing we were really and truly in love. I was overwhelmed, so I kept the photo to myself at first. I told Haley about it at our wedding reception, and we thought it would be a nice surprise to get one framed for you for Mother's Day." Lily's forehead creased with concern. "You're not mad we waited, are you?"

"Are you kidding? This is the best present I've ever received." *Other than West coming back.* Tabitha snuck a glance at him and for once hoped he could read her mind.

The tender smile that came to his lips told her he just might.

"The picture was taken at the dude ranch. See the way the trail curves into an S shape?" Lily pointed at the ground in the photo. "I can show you that exact spot the next time you're out at the ranch. Maybe you can pose with the boys in their stroller in the same spot, and we can re-create it."

"I *love* that idea," Haley said.

"Lub," Zane babbled. "Lub, lub, lub."

"That's right, baby." Tabitha ran her hand over her son's soft hair. "Love."

She was full to bursting with it. Forget Courtney Riddle's big plans for breakfast in bed. This had to be the best Mother's Day celebration in the history of motherhood. And it was all because of West. He'd done this. He'd put this crazy pajama party together.

For her.

"Thank you for all of this," she whispered in his ear later, when she and West were cutting the cake in the kitchen. "This is the perfect day. I really mean it. You were right, you know."

"I'm right about a lot of things," he teased. "Could you be more specific?"

"About what you said in Houston. It's okay that

I'm not like the Buckinghams…that I never felt like I fit into their world. I know they love me in their own way, and it's probably the only way they know how to love. They really do want the best for me. Lyle and Grace Buckingham will always be my parents. Alec will always be my brother." Tabitha swallowed around the knot of emotion that had formed in her throat. She wasn't sure she could get the rest out without breaking down in tears, but she had to say it. She wanted to remember this day and what it felt like to truly know her place in this world. "But the people right here in this house are my *family*. Zach and Zane. Lily and Haley."

She rested a hand on his firm chest, kissed him softly and smiled into his eyes. "And you too, West Fortune."

Then neither one of them said another word. They didn't have to. The moment spoke for itself, steeped in sweet buttercream and new traditions. But somewhere in the back of her head, Tabitha heard a still, small voice.

You still think your resistance to this man is crumbling? Oh, honey. It's already nothing but a pile of rubble at his boot-clad feet.

Chapter Ten

"West, you're going to spoil the boys if we don't stop shopping," Tabitha said the next morning as he crammed no less than half a dozen massive shopping bags from GreatStore into the trunk of her car.

She knew they should've taken West's pickup truck on this little shopping expedition. Or maybe even a horse trailer.

"There's no such thing as spoiling babies on their birthday. They're only turning one once." West pulled the list he'd been consulting all morning from the back pocket of his Wrangler jeans. The paper ruffled in the spring breeze as they stood in the parking lot.

Tabitha peeked at it, mentally checking off one item after another. "Surely you've gotten everything on there."

The list was sweet, really. West had compiled it after doing a copious amount of research on the parenting sites he'd been reading lately. Over the past few days, he'd done a deep dive on the best developmental toys for one-year-olds and pledged to buy them all… in duplicate. Two of everything—two sets of sensory blocks, two pop-a-ball push toys, two zoo-themed wooden activity cubes, and the list went on. Tabitha had no idea where they were going to put it all. He'd even bought the boys a ball pit—assembly required, which would no doubt be a treat that would keep them up late the night before the party. At least Tabitha had managed to talk him into getting only one of those.

"It's a lot, I know." West tucked the list back into his pocket. He removed his Stetson to rake a hand through his hair and then jammed the hat back on his head. Tabitha bit back a smile thinking about the matching baby cowboy hats currently occupying one of the shopping bags in her trunk. "I'm just excited about their birthday."

Tabitha had a feeling there was a lot more on his mind than simple excitement. Enthusiasm didn't require a printed list that had been cross-referenced across three different websites. "I know you are, but maybe there's something else going on here."

"We forgot the board books. Damn, I knew we'd missed something." West turned back toward the store.

Tabitha grabbed hold of his elbow and reeled him back toward her, like he was one of the calves he'd roped during his days as a ranch hand in hiding. "Whoa there, cowboy. We've done enough damage at Great-Store. Let's go to Remi's Reads. Afterward, maybe we can grab lunch at the Cowgirl Café since Lily and Asa are watching the boys."

"Sounds good." West nodded, but he still had that glazed look in his eyes that he always got when he was thinking about something else. Tabitha had seen that expression countless times, usually the night before a big jury trial. In this case, she suspected his mind was spinning with tricycles and other assorted baby paraphernalia.

She dipped her head to catch his gaze. "But first, I want you to know that you don't need to make up for the time you've been away. You're here now. The boys adore you. They're not even going to remember that you missed the first eleven months of their life."

West swallowed. She could see his Adam's apple move up and down his muscular neck. "Is my guilty conscience that obvious?"

"Yes, counselor, it is." Tabitha held her pointer finger and thumb a fraction of an inch apart. "Just a little bit."

"Kids with involved fathers have better overall emotional well-being," he said, and the underlying sorrow in his tone as he parroted one of the parenting articles he'd read made her want to cave and go back inside GreatStore for another ball pit.

"West, the twins have that. You're *here*." And he wasn't going anywhere. Wasn't that what he kept saying?

They still hadn't figured out a permanent arrangement or even discussed their future as a family, but she had stopped wondering if she might wake up in the morning and find him gone. All this time, she'd been holding her breath, waiting for the inevitable freak-out once reality sank in and West realized the lifelong implication of being the father of twins. The man who'd never wanted children to begin with was a daddy. Times two.

Tabitha hadn't fully recognized that the joy she felt upon his return had been tempered with an underlying fear that he'd bolt at the first sign of spit-up or a dirty diaper. Loving babies when they were clean and cuddly and smelled like baby powder was easy. But in real life, those moments were few and far between. It wasn't until after the Mother's Day surprise party yesterday that she'd finally begun to breathe a little easier.

West nodded. "You're right. I'm here now." Then he flashed her one of his crooked smiles that she loved so much. "But I still want to stop by Remi's Reads for those board books."

"Super, but then I'm cutting you off from parenting magazines. At least until we find a place for all of these gifts." Had they gotten enough wrapping paper and tape? They were going to be wrapping presents after the twins went to bed from now until the party next weekend.

"Yoo-hoo! Tabitha!"

A chirpy voice rang out behind them, and she didn't need to turn around to know who it was.

"Ugh," she muttered.

West's gaze drifted over her shoulder, no doubt landing on Courtney Riddle and her eyelash extensions flapping in the breeze. "What's wrong? Who is that?"

"One of the moms in my playgroup. She can be a bit of a mean girl, but overall she's harmless," Tabitha said under her breath as Courtney came bustling toward them pushing a shopping cart. Her twin girls sat in the cart's double-wide child seat area, dressed to the nines in matching floral dresses with massive bows in their hair. Just like always.

No bow, no go. That was Courtney's motto for her girls when it came to going out in public. Tabitha wouldn't have been surprised if the phrase turned out to be their very first words.

"Howdy, you two." The woman gave Tabitha a loud, smacking air kiss beside each cheek before turning her gaze on West. "Lookie, here. If it isn't Mr. Chatelaine himself, West Fortune."

She shoved her hand toward him, wiggling her hot-pink manicure. "Courtney Riddle. I'm a dear friend of Tabitha's. We met while she was all alone and pregnant, bless her heart."

Tabitha could see West's jaw clench as he shook her hand. "It's a pleasure to meet you."

"The pleasure is all mine. What are you two doing here?" She craned her neck to see inside the back of Tabitha's car. "And where are those precious twins of yours?"

"We're shopping for Zach and Zane's birthday," Tabitha said, being extra careful not to mention the party. As much as she'd come to rely on the playgroup moms, Courtney was the last person she wanted to invite into her home. "My sisters are watching the boys."

"Oh, that's a shame. I thought perhaps you'd called that nanny I told you about. I know it's been such a struggle for you to keep up with work without any help at home." She picked an invisible spot of lint off the Peter Pan collar of one of the twin's dresses.

West's jaw clenched again, this time so hard that

Tabitha was pretty sure she heard his teeth clang together.

Oblivious, Courtney turned her smile on him. "That was such a lovely party in the park the other day. The sheriff certainly seems thrilled to have you back. So have you made things permanent yet?"

What?

Was the nosy mom asking if they'd run off to the chapel and gotten married the second he'd come back from the dead?

Tabitha's face went as hot as the Texas sun in high summer. "Courtney, West and I—"

Her voice drifted off. *West and I what, exactly?* She still had no clue how to complete that sentence. Not that it was any business of Courtney's.

Courtney flicked her wrist. "I mean with the prosecutor's office, of course. Everyone is just dying to have you back there, West. Chatelaine needs you, good sir."

Tabitha and West hadn't discussed the sheriff's job offer for days. She'd actually allowed herself not to think about it after the lunch at the country club in Houston. That day had seemed like something of a turning point. But now here it was—the job offer of West's dreams—thrust right back to the forefront of Tabitha's mind, thanks to her playgroup nemesis.

"Nothing official," he said. "I'm still mulling over my options."

Tabitha's heart sank, despite every effort to remind herself how present West had been since he'd gotten back. Deep down, she'd even started to believe he was going to turn the job down.

Why was this decision taking so long?

"Well, good for you. You've been away an awful long while. No sense rushing into a serious commitment." Courtney's eyes flitted over hers, as if mentally blessing her poor, sad heart yet again.

Why did it feel like they were no longer talking about a job?

"We should get going," Tabitha said crisply. "We still have a lot of birthday errands to run."

Courtney gave her heart an exaggerated pat. "Oh, how sweet. Don't let me keep you. Will we see you at playgroup tomorrow, Tabitha? We missed you last week. Didn't we, girls?"

The twins swiveled their big blue eyes toward Tabitha.

Confession: Tabitha had skipped playgroup last week on purpose. She'd told herself there was no reason to go since she was so preoccupied with West's return. But in truth, she simply hadn't been ready to face the questions that Courtney and the others were surely waiting with bated breath to ask. It was one thing to admit to her sisters that she didn't know where she and West stood, but there was no way she was going to have that conversation with anyone else, least of all Courtney Riddle.

"Sure, I'll be there," Tabitha said, purely because it was the easiest way to extricate herself from the current third degree in progress.

"Wonderful. See you tomorrow, then. Toodle-loo," Courtney chirped, and then she hiked her designer handbag up further on her shoulder and aimed her shopping cart toward the GreatStore entrance.

Tabitha sighed the second she was out of earshot. "I told you. She's…a lot."

"Yeah." West let out a laugh, but it didn't quite meet his eyes. "Bless her heart."

Four toddler board books plus one adult-sized tome on raising multiples later, Tabitha and West exited the bookstore and nearly plowed straight into Freya Fortune on the sidewalk.

Hmm, Tabitha thought, *this must be the day for awkward, accidental run-ins*. Maybe they should've stayed home and shopped online instead of venturing out into the world at large.

She immediately chastised herself. Freya seemed like a genuinely nice, albeit lonely, person. The total and complete opposite of Courtney, whose flippant comments about West and commitment had thrown Tabitha for a loop. He hadn't seemed quite like himself since they'd bumped into her in the GreatStore parking lot, either. They'd been having such fun earlier, shopping for gifts and party decorations for the twins. But now things between them felt off, and Tabitha didn't like it. Not one bit.

It was probably just her imagination. She really shouldn't let Courtney get under her skin. Somehow that woman knew just what to say to tap into Tabitha's deepest insecurities. And to top it off, now she was going to have to show up at playgroup tomorrow. Oh, joy.

But she didn't need to think about that right now.

Tomorrow was another day, and Freya was standing right in front of them looking a bit shaken. Her sleek hairstyle wasn't as polished as usual, and there were worry lines around her eyes. Tabitha hoped she hadn't followed their advice about trying to track down her long-lost daughter and gotten bad news.

"Freya, are you okay?" she asked gently.

The older woman stumbled backward after their near collision in the doorway of the bookstore, and West took hold of her shoulders to steady her. "Careful, there. Let's go sit down somewhere for a few minutes. You look like you could use someone to talk to."

Again.

West aimed a meaningful glance at Tabitha. She knew precisely what he was thinking, because the same thought was spinning through her mind as well. Their encounters with Freya seemed to be getting progressively stranger.

"West." Freya blinked. "Tabitha! I'm so happy to see you. Sorry for bumping into you like that. I'm afraid I'm a little frazzled today."

"No worries at all," West said as he steered her toward one of the park benches that lined the streets of downtown Chatelaine.

Old wagon wheels served as armrests, with crossed pickaxes etched onto a metal plate on the bench's backrest—an homage to the town's mining history. Freya took a seat in the center of the bench and Tabitha sat down beside her.

West crouched down and smiled up at his stepgranny. "Anything in particular on your mind, Freya?"

The older woman folded her hands in her lap, unfolded them and folded them again. Clearly, something was wrong.

"There is, actually." She nodded, and then dropped her voice to a loud whisper. "I think someone is following me."

Tabitha looked around, but the street was mostly empty and quiet. It was the middle of the day on a Monday, and this was Chatelaine. Anyone trying to follow Freya would've stuck out like a sore thumb.

"Not now. At least I don't think so. I haven't seen her since I left my motel a little bit ago." Freya let out a breath.

"So it's a woman who's following you?" West asked in as calm a voice as Tabitha had ever heard him use. He was so great at this. His years of advocating for crime victims and questioning witnesses certainly showed.

"Maybe not following. Maybe just...*watching* me, somehow?" Freya shook her head. "I can't be sure. It's that new young woman in town. Her name is Morgana Mills. Do either of you know her?"

Tabitha shook her head. "Bea might have mentioned her once or twice, but I've never met her."

"Unless we crossed paths at the picnic last week, I haven't met her either," West said.

"She's a maid at the Chatelaine Motel where I'm staying." Freya gestured toward the tail end of the downtown area, where the old motor lodge stood just off the beaten path.

West nodded. "I know the place."

Everyone in town knew the motel. It was as old-school as an establishment could possibly get, with slightly peeling exterior paint and rosebud-pink sinks and tubs in all the bathrooms. But it was clean and respectable, run by Hal Appleby, a kind widower who'd lived in Chatelaine all his life. Pretty much everyone who passed through town, both visitors and those who eventually ended up putting down roots, had stayed there at least once in their life.

"My room is on the first floor. It's one of the big ones with a kitchenette. I think Morgana's room is on the second floor, right above mine." Freya's mouth twisted. "Anyway, when I first wondered if she might be watching me, she didn't work there. I just kept bumping into her around town, and the next thing I knew, boom. She got a job at the very motel where I'm staying."

Tabitha wanted to be sensitive to Freya's feelings, but this entire thing seemed pretty far-fetched. "Do you think it might be just a coincidence? There really aren't that many places to stay in Chatelaine, and if she's new in town, she was probably looking for a job. I'm sure Hal jumped at the chance to get some extra help."

"I'm telling you there's something off about that girl," Freya insisted.

West regarded her thoughtfully. "Besides the fact that you get the feeling she's watching you?"

"Yes. I heard she's been asking people around town about the old silver mine collapse. Now why would a total stranger, a *newcomer*, be poking her nose into that? Hmm?" Freya crossed her arms and let out a huff.

Something seemed off about this entire exchange, but Tabitha couldn't put her finger on it.

"Who *is* this woman?" Freya demanded.

"Like I said, I don't know. But if I learned anything in all my time as prosecutor, it's that the truth always comes out." West rested his hand on Freya's knee and gave it a comforting pat. *"Always."*

She shot him a skeptical glance. He and Tabitha clearly weren't making her feel any better about the mysterious Morgana.

"I have to go," Freya said, standing up abruptly.

"Right now?" Tabitha asked, but the older woman was already in motion, tearing past West, who was still crouching in front of the bench.

He rocked backward on the heels of his cowboy boots as she bustled into a nearby shop. Then he stood, brushed off his hands and narrowed his gaze in the direction where his step-granny had just disappeared.

Tabitha gathered the bags from the bookstore and came to stand beside him. "That was odd, wasn't it?"

"Very," he said flatly.

"Do you think she's just confused? Freya can be a bit eccentric, but she usually seems as sharp as a tack for a woman who's pushing ninety." Besides, it was Elias who'd had the idea to make all of his grandchildren's most fervent wishes come true. Not Freya. She was simply here in Chatelaine to do her late husband's bidding and bring the family back together.

Wasn't she?

"I don't think she's confused, but I do have a theory." West's gaze fixed on hers, and his lips pressed together in a hard line. He didn't look at all like he was turning over some vague idea in his head. He looked more like a man who'd just made up his mind with absolute certainty. "I've met all sorts of people in my day."

"And?" Tabitha prompted.

A muscle in West's jaw ticked. "And Freya Fortune is hiding something."

Chapter Eleven

"So I was thinking of going to playgroup with you today." West closed the book he was reading—*Double The Pleasure: Raising Twins*—and set it on top of his ever-growing stack of parenting books on the end table beside the sofa.

Tabitha blinked. "You what?"

"Isn't your moms-of-multiples playgroup today? You told your friend Courtney you'd be there." West reached for his coffee.

Sunshine streamed through the front windows of the cottage, and beyond the sheer curtains, he could see Betty Lawford sneak a glance at him as she trimmed her roses. She'd been doing that a lot lately. If she didn't give it a rest, she wouldn't have any roses left.

West waved at her, and she waved back.

He and Tabitha had just spent the early morning hours getting the boys changed and fed and then changed again. Now they were down for a short nap, giving the adults a few minutes to regroup. And to play nice with the nosy neighbors, apparently. What could it hurt? West was back in Chatelaine to stay. Betty might as well get used to it.

"So, about playgroup?" he asked again.

West and Tabitha had mulled over the strange encounter with Freya over dinner last night and hadn't managed to figure out what was going on there, leaving his mind to wander back to the issue of playgroup and the mean-girl mom he'd met in the GreatStore parking lot.

Not that he'd particularly enjoyed that little encounter.

Tabitha let out a nervous laugh. "First of all, I'm not sure I'd call Courtney my friend, exactly. It's more like we coexist in playgroup together."

No surprise there. West hadn't gotten the impression they were close. "And second?"

"It's usually just moms." Tabitha shrugged. "We started out as a sort of support group during our pregnancies. We all met in a special childbirth class for mothers of multiples. Twins and triplets are considered high-risk pregnancies, so the hospital offered a special class just for us. We started meeting outside of class for smoothies. Then, once all of us had our babies, we decided to keep getting together once a week."

West chose his next words carefully. Tabitha was a grown woman, and this was really none of his business. She'd been handling things on her own for nearly two years. But Courtney Riddle had rubbed him entirely the wrong way yesterday, and he couldn't shake the feeling that there was a reason Tabitha had skipped her weekly playgroup last week.

"Can I ask why?" He dropped his gaze to his coffee

cup. "Because correct me if I'm wrong, but you don't seem to enjoy it much."

"It's fine. Honestly. Most of the moms are perfectly lovely, and Courtney—" Tabitha rolled her eyes "—is just Courtney. I don't let her get to me. It's nice for the boys to have friends."

West held her gaze until she looked away, focusing on some invisible spot in the distance. When she did, his throat went thick. He'd been thinking about the exchange with Courtney all morning, wondering why Tabitha would want to spend any time at all with someone who seemed to be interjecting little digs into the conversation at her expense.

That didn't seem like the woman he knew. She valued her independence. She hated when the Buckinghams treated her that way, so West couldn't figure out why she'd willingly let somebody else talk down to her.

But now he realized why. Playgroup wasn't just about the twins. Zach and Zane weren't the only ones who needed friends and a support system. Tabitha did too. She'd been lonely.

He blamed himself. He'd left her high and dry, pregnant and alone. Perhaps that's why Courtney's faux sympathy had gotten to him. The things she'd said had been true.

We met while she was all alone and pregnant.

He felt sick just thinking about it. It hadn't been intentional. He'd had no idea she was pregnant, but facts were facts.

"I don't want to intrude. I just thought it might be fun

seeing the boys interacting with other kids their age. Forget I mentioned it," he said, not wanting to push. Things between them had gotten easier. More natural. But he didn't want to disturb the delicate balance they'd managed to find over the past week and a half.

West needed to accept that there were certain things he'd never be able to do, no matter how hard he tried. He'd never be able to be there for the birth of his sons. He'd never be able to go back in time and rub Tabitha's feet after a hard day of working all through her pregnancy. The prospect of raising twins on her own couldn't have been easy.

He didn't want her to feel that way anymore, and it was time to do everything in his power to make sure she didn't. Which meant he needed to have a chat with Sheriff Cooper.

West couldn't take the job. He didn't even want it. In all honesty, he wasn't sure how his professional life would look going forward. But he did know that working as the county prosecutor was no longer a good fit. He needed to close that door firmly behind him, once and for all.

He turned toward Tabitha. "Tabs, about the sheriff—"

But she wasn't paying attention. Her eyebrows were drawn together, and her pretty bow lips were pursed, like she was turning something over in her head. Overthinking again.

Her gaze flitted toward his, eyes sparkling with sudden determination. "You know what? I think Zach and Zane would love it if you joined us."

It was the last thing he'd expected her to say.

His head drew back to search her expression. She seemed serious. "Really?"

"Yes, and why shouldn't you get to see how nicely the boys play with their friends? It will be a nice change of pace for playgroup. It's not like there's a *no dads allowed* rule or anything. It's just never come up before." She stood and began gathering the twins' things, packing them away in their diaper bag.

In went a stack of disposable diapers, baby wipes, hand sanitizer, a Tupperware container of Cheerios and two fresh changes of baby clothes. Then she grabbed a few bottles, burp cloths, baby sunscreen and two tiny shade hats. She glanced around for more.

West had packed less stuff when he'd returned from his trip to the great heavenly beyond. Just how long did playgroup last, exactly?

"You're sure about this? I don't want to intrude." He followed her as she flitted around the living room and kitchen area and held up his hands. The chat about his future job prospects would have to wait. Tabitha had suddenly morphed into a woman on a mission.

"Absolutely. Like I said, Zach and Zane will love it." She brightened, and all at once, West was struck by how much she'd opened up to him since he'd been back.

Things were changing. She trusted him again. He'd turned back up in her life out of the blue after breaking her heart, and she'd welcomed him into her home. Her life. Her children's lives.

He didn't deserve any of it. No amount of resolve on his part could change the past. What's done was done.

But maybe, just maybe, having her welcome him back into her heart wasn't a pipe dream, after all.

"And you know what?" she asked, her pretty bow-shaped lips curving into a smile so tender and gentle that it seemed to reach inside West's chest and soothe the regret that he'd carried back home with him. His knapsack might've been as light as air, but the baggage he'd been toting around since his childhood had nearly broken him. For years.

The more he got to know his sons, the more he began to believe that he might finally be capable of setting that baggage down. Oh, how he wanted to.

"What?" he murmured, reaching down to touch her face. She was so damn beautiful that it took his breath away. He'd thought he'd remembered everything about her—every detail of her flawless face, every variety of her laughter, every curve that he'd once kissed, touched, adored...

West had dwelled on all those things for so long, wanting...hoping...remembering... He'd never expected to be surprised or caught off guard by the way he felt around her. But memory was just time caught in a bottle. This was different. This was real, and it was everything he wanted and more.

He wanted to kiss her so bad that it hurt, but he'd made her a promise and he intended to keep it. She needed time and space, and he wasn't about to push. So he gave her cheek one last caress before tucking a lock of her hair behind her ear and then shoving his hands into his pockets.

"I'd love it if you came, too," she said, and West thought that maybe his brother had been right.

Maybe they could figure things out. Maybe they could be a real family. Maybe West Fortune had truly come back to life.

An hour later, Tabitha stood beside West on Courtney Riddle's front porch, wondering why on earth she'd agreed to bring him to playgroup.

She'd lost her head for a minute. That had to be it. His interest in the boys and their friends had tugged at her heartstrings and hit her square in the chest. And then he'd given her that look—that certain, specific tilt of his head that reminded her so much of her boys.

Sometimes the expression on his face bore such a resemblance to Zach and Zane that her breath caught in her throat. Technically, it was the reverse—the twins looked like their dad, not the other way around. She was just so used to seeing their tiny faces every day, with their pudgy cheeks and bright blue eyes. They'd become her entire world, and West's memory was just that. A memory.

Not so much anymore.

Then he'd towered over her in all his masculine, cowboy glory, and the joy in his eyes when she'd said yes, he could come, nearly swept her clear off her feet.

Who are you kidding? West Fortune swept you off your feet ages ago, and your toes still haven't touched the ground.

When he'd reached a hand toward her face, Tabitha had thought he was going to cup her cheek and run his thumb gently across her bottom lip like he used to do when he wanted to kiss her. Her mouth had tingled in anticipation. But instead, he'd simply tucked a wayward lock of hair behind her ear.

She was pretty sure she'd had a dollop of pureed apricots from the twins' breakfast stuck somewhere in her bangs, but West hadn't seemed to notice. He'd always had a way of looking at her that made her feel like the most beautiful woman in the world. It was comforting to know that some things never changed, even when everything in their lives had gone so topsy-turvy.

Tabitha took a deep breath now and tried not to think about his warm, solid presence standing beside her on Courtney's porch. This was about the twins, not her—and definitely not about the sparks that had suddenly seemed to be flying all over the living room earlier. Her little house was far too small. West was always *right there*. That was the real problem.

Sure it is, her subconscious screamed. Even so, getting out of the cottage had suddenly seemed like the best idea she'd ever heard. She lifted her free hand and pressed the doorbell with what might've been excessive force.

West gave her a sideways glance, but she kept her attention glued straight ahead. How was she going to explain his presence? For all Courtney's bragging about the virtues of a nuclear family, Tabitha had never once witnessed a father darken the door of their weekly play date.

The door flew open, and she flinched. At first Courtney didn't notice anything unusual. Her head was turned, and she was saying something to another mom. When she finally swiveled to face them, it almost seemed like an afterthought.

But then her gaze landed on West, holding a twin in each arm.

Courtney's mouth dropped open an almost comical amount. Her eyes slowly moved over to Tabitha. "Tabitha, hi. I see you've brought company."

"I hope it's okay that I'm joining this week," West said, all politeness and charm.

Their host practically melted on the spot. "Of course. We're happy to have you. Come on in."

More astonishment ensued as they stepped inside Courtney's cavernous living room. The moms couldn't have been more stunned to find a dad among their midst, particularly one who'd recently come back from the dead. West got the boys settled in the middle of the play area and after a flurry of introductions, he almost had a handle on which babies belonged to which moms. As the kids played and West chatted with the other parents, Tabitha realized she was actually having a good time.

"Can I help with anything?" she asked Courtney when it was nearly time for snacks. Much like her daughters' meticulous bow collection, Courtney kept play hour carefully organized. Healthy snacks were served to the kids at the half-hour mark, on the dot.

Courtney's gaze drifted toward West, who was helping Zach toddle around with a walker wagon.

"That would be great. It seems your man has everything under control."

Her man.

Happiness coursed through Tabitha. Was West hers again? Did she want him to be? "Whatever you need. Just let me know."

"Could you grab the ice pops out of the freezer in the kitchen? I need to change Dotsy's diaper real quick." Courtney scooped one of her twins into her arms. "I'll be right there to get the napkins."

"No problem."

Tabitha wiggled her fingertips in a little wave to West, mouthed she'd be right back and made her way to the kitchen.

As many times as she'd been in the woman's palatial home, Tabitha never failed to marvel at how spacious it was. The kitchen was self-contained, instead of simply divided from the living area by a countertop, like Tabitha's home had been designed. A sleek island stood in the center of the space and a massive stainless-steel refrigerator took up a good portion of the opposite wall. A collection of cheery, posed family portraits were stuck to the front of it with alphabet magnets.

It took her a minute to figure out the fancy fridge. When she opened the freezer door, the ice pops were right there in the front—homemade, of course, in a variety of fruity flavors on colorful, toddler-friendly plastic handles. Had she expected anything less from Super Mom?

But as she removed the tray of freeze pops, Tabitha

spied a familiar yellow box with red lettering situated directly behind it. Her eyes went wide, and she nearly dropped the ice pops in her astonishment.

Frozen waffles?

No way. This couldn't be happening. It just wasn't possible.

Oh, but it was. And not only was there a box of preservative-laden frozen waffles in Courtney's freezer, but they were the brand that Tabitha preferred. The *same exact* waffles that had prompted Courtney to lecture her about the evils of processed foods in the freezer aisle at GreatStore on the one-year anniversary of West's death.

Tabitha couldn't believe her eyes. She just stood there, reveling in the sight of a simple box of frozen breakfast food. Bless Courtney's heart, the waffles weren't even whole grain. Clearly, the queen of the playgroup wasn't quite as perfect as she wanted everyone to believe.

"You're really lucky, you know."

Tabitha nearly jumped out of her skin at the sound of Courtney's voice behind her. She slammed the freezer door closed, turned around and did her best to pretend she hadn't noticed anything amiss.

But they both knew she had. The look on Courtney's face said at all. For once, her perfectly lined lips weren't curved into a condescending smile. She simply looked tired…every bit as exhausted as Tabitha felt after a full day of juggling her web design business with taking care of Zach and Zane.

"Excuse me?" Tabitha said. She must've misheard things. Surely Courtney hadn't just called her lucky.

"I said you're really lucky. None of the other dads have even thought about coming to playgroup. My husband sure hasn't. This would be the last place he'd want to be on a weekday morning."

And all at once, Tabitha understood. All of Courtney's posturing hadn't been a show for her and the other moms. It had simply been the other mom's way of convincing herself that her life was as flawless and wonderful as she wanted it to be. Underneath it all, she was just as overwhelmed as the rest of them were. Maybe if Tabitha hadn't been so mired down herself, she would've seen it.

She probably should've responded to the "lucky" comment, but instead, the words that popped out of her mouth were ones she'd been holding back for days. "It was you gossiping about West and me at the picnic, wasn't it?"

Courtney took a deep, pained breath and closed her eyes.

"I knew it." Tabitha set down the ice pops with a clunk. "Why, Courtney? I don't understand."

"I'm sorry. I really am. It's just that sometimes I get so…" She paused, and Tabitha had no idea what was coming next. *"…lonely."*

"Lonely? *You?*" Tabitha swallowed back her disbelief.

"Yes. Raising twins is hard. You know that even better than the rest of us, because up until now you've been doing it all by yourself. And the crazy thing is, I actually envy you."

"Courtney, trust me. I get lonely too—more than you could possibly imagine." It hurt Tabitha to admit it, but it was the truth.

Lately, though, she hadn't felt lonely at all. She liked having West stay at the house far more than she was ready to admit.

"But you were alone." Courtney's head gave a little shake, and tears swam in her eyes. "Being lonely by yourself is one thing, but being lonely when you're in a relationship is another."

Oh. So all the barbs and little digs had been about Courtney's marriage. They'd had nothing to do with Tabitha or West at all. Not really.

"Courtney, I'm really sorry." She had every reason to be angry at Courtney. The woman had made her life miserable on more than one occasion, but Tabitha couldn't bring herself to feel anything but empathy.

Even when West had broken her heart and told her he never wanted children, she'd never doubted the depth of his devotion toward her. She knew West cared about her even when he disappeared into his work and resisted talking about his childhood. He'd never stopped loving her. Deep down, she'd always known that's why he hadn't fought her when she'd broken off their engagement. She'd wanted him to fight so badly. Wanted him to kick and scream and rail against the idea of being apart. Instead, he'd quietly agreed and walked away...

Because he loved her. And when you cared deeply

for someone, you wanted them to be happy. West had wanted her to have everything she'd ever dreamed of—the kids, the family, the white picket fence.

Tabitha had been alone in the dark days that followed, but she'd never felt unloved. That's why it had been so hard to let go of West's memory. That's why she'd still worn his ring on a chain around her neck. He'd been gone, but their love had remained.

Maybe it still did.

"I'm the one who's sorry." Courtney gave her a wistful smile. "Can you ever forgive me?"

"Of course. And if you ever need to talk about things, I'm here, okay?" Tabitha nodded toward the freezer. "But if you show up at my house, I'm definitely serving you frozen waffles."

"I'd like that. Those things are so good," Courtney said as she dabbed at the corners of her eyes with a napkin.

"*So* good," Tabitha agreed.

The other mom sniffed, squared her shoulders and blew out a breath. It was strange seeing her so vulnerable, and Tabitha wondered if she realized it made her seem far more beautiful than her lush eyelashes and expensive clothes.

"Shall we get these ice pops out there before they melt?" She held one up. It was shaped like a strawberry, attached to an easy-to-hold plastic ring for babies and toddlers. Courtney really was great at this sort of thing.

"Let's do it." Courtney straightened a stack of polka-dot napkins, then paused. "Can I say one more thing, though?"

Tabitha nodded warily. What now?

"He still loves you, you know."

"I—" Tabitha's mouth went dry as her heart began to pound in her throat.

"He really does. Can't you see it? Because all the rest of us do. It's written all over his face every time he looks at you and every time he looks at those boys of yours." Courtney's smile turned a little less sad and a little more genuine. "I know things are complicated because he's been gone so long, but you really are the lucky one. If he still loves you and you love him, maybe that's all that really matters. Perhaps it's really just as simple as that."

Right then and there, a piece of Tabitha's heart melted along with the ice pops in her hands.

Perhaps it is.

Chapter Twelve

West had never seen a woman look so much like a spooked horse as Tabitha did the following evening as she was headed out for a girls' night out with her sisters.

"Are you sure about this? Because I don't have to go. It's just Ladies' Night at the Chatelaine Bar and Grill. It happens every week." She gnawed on her bottom lip as she switched her handbag from one shoulder to the other.

"And when was the last time you, Haley and Lily actually went to Ladies' Night together?" West plucked Zane from his highchair.

The twins were in the middle of dinner. Zach's plate was nearly empty, but thus far, Zane hadn't done much but fuss and smear his food around.

"Well…" Tabitha pulled a face. "Technically, we've never been. But—"

"No buts." West held up a hand, and little Zane mimicked him, doing the same in West's arms. "You're going. I can handle the boys on my own. I promise."

She deserved a night out with her sisters. What's more, she needed it. Tabitha never stopped doing for others, and West knew how badly she'd wanted to reconnect with Haley and Lily, now that they were adults.

Her sisters loved spending time with the twins. That much was obvious. But the girls needed alone time, too—time to nurture their newfound bond. West could certainly appreciate that, after having been isolated from his family for nearly two years. He'd been in contact with Camden daily since his return to Chatelaine and was eager for Bear to turn up back in town so they could reconnect.

"You know, I really do think I'm getting the hang of this fatherhood thing," he said as he wiped orange sweet potato from Zane's chubby fingers.

"Don't say that. As soon as you do, something will no doubt spin wildly out of control." Tabitha dropped her handbag on the table by the front door. "Trust me. A few months ago, I was all caught up with work and the babies stopped teething, and I was so delighted about all of it that I told Bea I'd finally gotten things under control at home. Then, the next day, all three of us caught a stomach bug. It was a nightmare. You have no idea."

West carried Zane to the door, took Tabitha's bag off the table and replaced it on her shoulder. "Bye, sweetheart. I want you to have a good time with your sisters tonight. The twins and I will be just fine. If anyone gets a stomach bug, you'll be the first to know. Cell phones exist for this very reason."

West was determined not to call her, though. He was the twins' father, not their babysitter. He should be capable of watching his own kids by himself for a few hours while their mother had time to herself.

Tabitha's eyes narrowed. "You're really sure about this?"

"One hundred percent." He gave her the most tender look in his arsenal. How would he ever feel like a read dad unless he acted like one? The past few weeks had meant more to West than he ever could've imagined, but they'd almost been like a dream. If this was going to be his life, he wanted to be *all* in. "I need you to let me do this, Tabs. Not just for you, but for me, too. Okay?"

That seemed to convince her.

"Okay." She nodded, rose up on tiptoe and brushed her lips against the corner of his mouth. The nervousness in her expression faded into something else… something that felt a little bit like adoration. "And maybe later when I get home, we can chat about a few things."

That sounded promising.

West felt the corner of his mouth tug into a grin. "Yeah?"

"Yeah. I think it's time." Her mouth was still just a whisper away from his.

If he hadn't had a baby in his arms, he might've buried his hands in her hair and given her a proper kiss goodbye.

But they weren't there yet, anyway. She still had his ring on her finger, but it had been placed there as part of a ruse. West longed to put it there himself, like he'd done all those years ago. To slide it in place with a promise.

It's time. Tonight things would change. They were finally ready to be a real family. She'd stopped waiting for him to bolt like a runaway horse. He could see it in her eyes.

"So do I, darlin'," he said, and then their sweet goodbye was interrupted by Zane emitting an earsplitting squeal.

Tabitha kissed the baby on the forehead then waved at Zach, and West managed to usher her out the door before she could change her mind and insist on staying.

"Okay, kiddos. It's just us," West said as he clicked the door shut behind her. "Boys' night."

Zach grinned and shoved one of his tiny fists into his mouth. Zane seemed a little less enthusiastic about the whole affair. He went stiff in the crook of West's elbow and started to fuss.

"Come on, buddy. It's okay. Daddy's here," West soothed.

"Dadadaddadada." Zach banged on the tray of his highchair and kicked his legs.

"Dada," Zane said in a pitifully small voice.

"That's right. We're good, aren't we?"

West ran his hand over Zane's slender back, and for a second, he thought he'd managed to calm the baby down. But then Zane scrunched his face and began to cry in earnest—loud, wracking sobs that shook his entire body. Zach watched his brother, eyes as big as saucers, and then he joined in the chorus, screaming at the top of his little lungs.

Panic shot through West. What was happening? Tabitha probably hadn't even made it to the Chatelaine Bar and Grill yet, and already things were going off the rails.

It's just a few tears. Babies cry. No big deal. He'd certainly heard his sons cry before. Just not quite this loud. Or this urgently. And not both at the same time, as if they'd decided to gang up on him the second their mother had finally decided he could be trusted to look after them on his own.

"First things first. Let's get you out of that chair, Zach."

West put Zane down in his crib and then dashed back to the kitchen to get Zach. In the split second it took him to carry Zach to the nursery, Zane's cheeks had turned beet red, and his entire face was wet with some awful combination of tears and mucus.

He picked him up, held Zane close against his chest and took calm, slow breaths while he tried to remember what the parenting books said about crying babies. He ran through the list in his head—something about walking, rocking and singing. He couldn't remember, so he tried all three, but nothing worked. The baby's diaper was clean, but he was inconsolable.

Zach stood watching West's efforts from his crib, bouncing on his toes until he too, began to fuss. He still needed to be cleaned up from dinner. West had planned on bathing them together, getting them dressed in a pair of their cute, matching PJs and then reading them a bedtime story. It was a routine he'd practiced and perfected since he'd been living on Tabitha's sofa. But tonight, it just wasn't working.

Nothing was.

Breathe. Just breathe, he thought, but he wasn't sure if he was talking to the babies or himself.

You can do this. Tabitha has done it on her own for a year. You can handle two crying babies for a single evening.

West wasn't going to call her, either. He wanted to prove to himself that he was father material. If not now, when? He was just feeling a little out of his element, that's all, like a newborn colt trying to stand on wobbly legs. He'd simply stay calm, get the house cleaned up and stick to the routine. He'd figure out a way to mollify Zane, and when Tabitha came home later tonight, the boys would be as happy as two peas in a pod.

West took a deep breath and reminded himself how much he loved his family, how much he wanted this to work. How for nineteen long months he'd prayed every night for another chance to make things right with Tabitha. And when he'd finally made his way home, and found out he was a daddy, his very first thought was that it had all been worth it. All the days in the hot sun on the ranch. All the lonely nights. All the endless waiting…

He was home. He had a purpose beyond his wildest dreams. He'd overcome the lowest of lows, and at long last, he'd put the pain of his past behind him.

And then, just as West managed to talk himself back from the brink, things went from bad to worse.

Tabitha's cheeks hurt from smiling so much as she sat in the red leather banquette at the Chatelaine Bar and Grill with her sisters. She couldn't remember the last time she'd laughed this hard. Or loud.

And she couldn't even blame it on the bottle of good red wine in the center of the table, which was steeply discounted for Ladies' Night. Tabitha, Haley and Lily had each consumed only half a glass by the time their entrees arrived. They'd been too busy talking to get through more than a third of the bottle between them.

It felt good to joke around with her sisters. This was the sort of camaraderie she'd longed for when she'd first found out she was a triplet. She wished she had more time to spend with Lily and Haley—time that didn't involve juggling, changing and feeding two babies while also trying to keep up with the conversation. Time was a precious commodity when you were a mom to twins, though, and Tabitha knew better than to waste it. So she did her best to ignore her phone and focus on her sisters. If the boys needed anything, West would call or text. Staring at the tiny screen wasn't going to do her any good.

"So how are things going at home?" Lily asked, eyes bright in the dimly lit restaurant.

Hands down the nicest dining establishment in town, Chatelaine Bar and Grill featured dark wood paneling and rich leather accents. The walls were covered with framed, sepia-toned photographs and old maps of the mines that dotted the town's landscape. Authentic retro pans that miners had used to search for gold hung in an artistic arrangement over the bar. Tabitha had always loved the way the town embraced its history. The way the mines were still incorporated into everyday life in Chatelaine ensured that the miners who'd lost their lives were never forgotten.

"'How are things going at home?'" Tabitha regarded Lily. "Is that code for asking me how things are going with West?"

"Perhaps." Her sister's mouth twitched into a grin. "Okay, yes. It was absolutely code."

Haley leaned forward on the leather seat of the booth. "Yeah, tell us everything."

"I'm afraid there's nothing official to tell." Tabitha smiled into her wineglass. "Yet."

"Yet?" Lily's left eyebrow quirked upward as she swiveled her gaze toward Haley. "Did she just say 'yet'?"

"One hundred percent," Haley said with a nod.

Then both of Tabitha's sisters squealed in unison.

"You love him. I knew it!" Lily punctuated her statement with a stab of her fork.

Haley spread her arms out wide. "We *all* knew it."

"Shhh." Tabitha laughed and pressed a finger to her lips. "West still doesn't know it, and I'd really like him to hear it from me first."

"When are you going to tell him?" Lily added a dollop of butter to her baked potato.

"I think I'm going to tell him tonight. It's time. You guys were right. Once I started trying to take things one day at a time, West and I sort of found our way." She toyed with the napkin in her lap. "He still hasn't said anything about the job at the sheriff's office, but maybe that shouldn't be a deal-breaker. He's so good with the boys. I'm genuinely starting to believe we have a shot at being a family. If we really love each other and if he really loves Zach and Zane, we should be able to figure out the rest. Right?"

It felt so odd saying these things out loud. Tabitha had been working so hard to keep her feelings in check and temper her expectations where West was concerned. After all, he'd let her down before. He'd shattered her heart into a million pieces, and it had been so tempting to think he could just swoop back in and put it back together.

But she had the boys to think about now. Like a mama bear, she wouldn't let anyone or anything hurt them. The thought of their tender, innocent souls being rejected by a man who didn't believe he could ever be a father was too much to take.

West had changed, though. She'd seen it. It had happened right before her eyes, day by day. He'd committed himself to their little family, and she was tired of fighting the truth. Tired of waiting for the other shoe to drop, because what if it never did?

What then?

"Right," Lily said and pressed a hand to her heart. "Oh, sis. I'm so happy for you."

Haley nodded, but just as she was about to say something, the chime of a cell phone cut her off.

"Whose phone is that?" Lily fished around in her purse.

"It's mine." Tabitha glanced down at her device, where a notification from West lit up the small screen. "West is texting me."

"Aw, that's sweet." Haley reached for the bread-basket.

"I need to read it. He's alone with the boys for the first time. I'm sure things are fine..." Tabitha said, but no sooner had the words left her mouth than her heart stuttered to a stop.

West: I'm sorry. I don't know what to do. Zane won't stop crying. I've tried everything.

She frowned down at her phone. "He says Zane won't stop crying."

Her sisters exchanged a glance. Tabitha felt like she had cotton in her ears as the sounds of the restaurant faded into the background.

Haley reached over to rest a hand on Tabitha's fore-arm. "He's probably just feeling overwhelmed. He's not used to taking care of babies. My nephews are little angels, but they can be a handful every now and then."

"I'm sure you're right," Tabitha said, but the text message went blurry as her hand started to tremble.

West had been so insistent about wanting her to go out and have a good time. He wouldn't have texted her unless something was seriously wrong.

Don't panic. You can trust him. She knew she could. Wasn't that what she'd just been telling her sisters?

West knew how to comfort a crying baby. She'd watched him do it over and over again already, and it wasn't as if he didn't know how to keep calm in a crisis. Even when he'd been in the crosshairs of the

Mexican drug cartel, he'd had the presence of mind to fake his own death.

Something is wrong.

Tabitha took a deep breath. If she called him and sounded anything but confident, she'd make things worse. Besides, Zane had been fussy earlier too. He was probably just getting a cold or an ear infection, either of which would throw West for a loop. The boys had been perfectly healthy the entire time he'd been back. But Tabitha remembered how helpless she'd felt the first time one of the twins had gotten sick. She'd been terrified. That had to be what was going on.

"I'm going to text him back," she said as she tapped out a message.

Tabitha: Try not to worry. He might be coming down with something. Does he seem warm?

West: His face is red, and he's burning up. I thought it was because of all the crying.

Now they were getting somewhere. The baby almost surely had a fever.

Tabitha: Take his temperature. The baby thermometer is in the bathroom cabinet.

"Is everything okay?" Lily asked, gaze fixed on Tabitha's phone.

"He's checking Zane for fever."

It was fine, though. Babies and small children got

fevers all the time. A little Baby Tylenol would fix everything.

But then her phone chimed again, and the sound made Tabitha jump, as if she knew it wasn't going to be good news.

West: 104 degrees.

Things were most decidedly *not* fine.

Tabitha couldn't have made it back to the cottage faster if she'd teleported, yet West still felt as if he lived and died a thousand deaths in the time between when he'd taken Zane's temperature and the breathless moment she flew through the door.

A fever.

How had he not known to take the baby's temperature? If he'd had the first clue what he was doing…if he had any natural parental instincts at all…he would've known to check. It seemed so obvious in retrospect. Zane had been so fussy, and the more he'd cried, the redder his face became. When West held him against his chest and tried to rock him to sleep, the baby had been hot as a fire poker. Still, he'd somehow forgotten that children got fevers.

And then it had been too late. The baby had started shivering, and West knew he was in over his head. He'd been so sure he could handle things on his own, so eager to prove to himself that he was father material. Now Zane was burning up, and Tabitha would probably never trust him with the boys again.

Seriously? Acid churned in West's stomach. *That's what you're worried about right now?*

How selfish could he possibly be? Even now, when Zane should be first and foremost on his mind, West was thinking about himself. Bile rose to the back of his throat as the image of his dad's face swam in his mind.

Like father, like son.

The past had truly come home to roost. He knew all along it would only be a matter of time.

"West," Tabitha said, as she held a screaming Zane to her chest. Her voice barely registered in his consciousness. He scarcely remembered handing the baby over after she'd burst through the door a few moments earlier. *"West!"*

His head snapped up, and he realized Lily was there too. She had Zach cradled in one arm while she threw items into an overnight bag with her free hand.

"We need to take Zane to the hospital," Tabitha said in a startlingly calm voice. Her competency and ability to think straight in the middle of this crisis only made West feel worse. "Lily is going to take Zach home with her so she and Asa can watch him. Haley stayed back at the restaurant to pay the check."

"Good, good," West muttered as he raked a hand through his hair. Thank God. The actual adults were going to get everything under control so he couldn't ruin anything else. If she'd asked him to watch Zach while she took Zane to the ER, he wasn't sure he would've been able to say yes.

He shifted from one foot to the other while Tabitha kept looking at him, as if expecting more of a response.

He couldn't think with Zane screaming so loud. West felt each cry like a knife to the chest.

"Go get the keys. You're driving," Tabitha said, again in a serene tone that somehow seemed far more ominous than if she'd been hysterical.

West hoped she'd yell at him later. He deserved it. But now wasn't the time. They needed to get the baby to the hospital and get his fever down before…

Before what, exactly?

He grabbed the keys and squeezed them in his fist until the metal dug into his flesh. *Seizures? Unconsciousness? Brain damage?* Every terrible thing he'd read about fevers in the parenting books reared its ugly head as he rushed outside and held the back car door open for Tabitha.

She settled Zane into his car seat. He'd finally stopped screaming, which should've been a relief. But he was as listless as a wet rag, which terrified West right down to his core. Tabitha handled the baby quickly but tenderly, getting him safely strapped in for the short ride to South Texas County Hospital, located in the county seat near Chatelaine.

Then she slid in place next to the child in the backseat so she could be close to him on the way, and it wasn't until she was safely buckled in and West clicked the car door shut that her composure broke. If he hadn't turned his head for one last glimpse after he'd closed the door, he would've missed the quiver in Tabitha's chin and the way her eyes filled when she thought he wasn't looking.

In a night filled with regrets, that was the most shameful part of all.

West wasn't supposed to be making things harder. Tabitha shouldn't have to hide her feelings from him. A real father made things better, not worse. Then again, what did he really and truly know about being a dad?

Playing house...that's all you've been doing. You know that, right?

There was more to being a father than changing a few diapers and showing up at playgroup. Had he really thought that spending a few weeks on Tabitha's sofa would make them a family?

West tightened his grip on the steering wheel and steadfastly avoided looking at mother and child in the rearview mirror. He couldn't take it. He was an intruder in this scenario. He had been, all along.

Tabitha's heart was simply bigger than his. Always had been, always would be. She was a far better person than him, back before he'd disappeared, and that simple fact still held true. He'd endangered her life and left her pregnant, and when he'd swept back into Chatelaine on his proverbial white horse, the entire town called him a hero. They threw him a picnic in the park and offered him the keys to the freaking city. And West had bought into the spectacle, hook, line and sinker, when in reality, Tabitha had been the brave one.

She'd had no good reason to trust him anymore. She'd given herself to him, body and soul, and when the subject of children had come up, he'd all but used it as an excuse to cut and run. Yeah, he'd regretted it afterward, but the damage had been done. He'd broken their trust—not just damaged it, but set fire to it and watched it burn. And how had she responded when he'd strutted back into town?

By opening her home to him…and her bed.

And now West's only saving grace was that she'd stopped short of offering him her heart.

After Tabitha carried Zane into the emergency entrance of South Texas County Hospital, the hours that followed passed in a blur.

Upon their arrival, they were immediately whisked away to a bed in the ER, surrounded by a privacy curtain. Zane looked so helpless and tiny, surrounded by beeping monitors and medical equipment. There was barely room for Tabitha and West to squeeze beside him in two small chairs while the emergency nurse did a quick assessment.

Since West had been the one watching the baby, most of the nurse's questions were directed at him.

Is the child experiencing any confusion?

No.

Any vomiting?

No.

Any seizures, rash or trouble breathing?

No, no and no.

Tabitha began to breathe a little easier. Zane's IV drip already seemed to be working. He seemed calmer and less agitated than when they'd first administered the medication. Even his color was looking better.

She wasn't sure when exactly she'd first grabbed

hold of West's hand, but she squeezed it tight, pressing as much reassurance into the gesture as she could.

See? Everything is going to be fine.

His palm was stiff in her grasp, though. He offered her no reaction whatsoever. The look in his eyes seemed almost haunted.

Even two hours later, when the emergency physician gave them the good news that Zane could go home, West still seemed rattled.

"Little Zane is going to be just fine. He's got a monster of an ear infection. That's what was causing the fever. We've given him a big dose of intravenous antibiotics, plus a fever reducer and some fluids to ward off dehydration." The doctor ran a hand over Zane's head, smoothing back his wispy blond hair. "He's out like a light now. There's really no reason to admit him. I'm sure you'll all be much more comfortable at home."

West tensed beside Tabitha. "But what if his fever spikes again?"

"It shouldn't, now that we've got some medicine in him. I'm sending you home with some baby acetaminophen. For the next day or two, just follow the dosing schedule and it should stay under control. Cool washcloths on the forehead can help. Make sure to elevate his head while he's sleeping. That should decrease pressure on the ear and relieve some of the pain."

Tabitha nodded. "We can do that."

"I don't know." West pulled his hand away and crossed his arms. "Maybe he should at least spend the night. Just to be on the safe side."

"I know you're worried, but this is all completely

normal and natural. Babies are prone to getting ear infections because their immune systems are still underdeveloped. Their eustachian tubes are very small and horizontal, which makes it difficult for fluid to drain out of their ears. This isn't Zane's first ear infection, is it?" The doctor's eyebrows lifted as he focused on West.

"I... I don't know, actually," he said quietly.

Tabitha shook her head. "It's not. He had one a few months ago. So did his twin brother, Zach."

"That's what I thought. This isn't his first, and it certainly won't be his last. Ear infections peak around this age, and they usually last until the child is eight years old or so. Most of the time, they start with a stuffy nose, but they can also come on quick like this one did tonight." The doctor rested a hand on Zane's chest, rising and falling as he slept. "Try not to worry. Just get this little one home so you can all get some rest. You should schedule a follow-up with your regular pediatrician a few weeks down the road. If possible, I'd keep Zane separated from his twin for two or three days. The colds that cause ear infections can be mighty contagious."

Tabitha glanced up at West. "I'll see if Zach can stay with Lily for a couple more nights."

He nodded without meeting her gaze. "That's a good idea."

It took another hour to complete the discharge paperwork and get Zane home. Tabitha changed him into fresh pajamas, and he settled down in his crib right away, exhausted by the entire ordeal. She'd called Lily and Asa on the way back to the cottage, and they'd promised they were happy to take care of Zach. Haley had checked in too, and she said she'd pop over to pick up more of Zach's things the following day and take them over to the ranch where Lily and Asa lived.

Tabitha was dead on her feet by the time she dressed for bed. She and West obviously wouldn't be able to have that chat tonight. A discussion about their future shouldn't be rushed, especially when he was so clearly rattled by Zane's illness. He looked so drained as he sank onto the sofa and pulled off his boots, bowed by the weight of the world. His left shoulder sagged. Most of the time, the lingering effects of West's gunshot wound were all but invisible. But tonight, the man before her was battle-weary and broken down.

"I'm sorry, Tabs," he said in a voice as soft as the velvety darkness. "So sorry. This was all my fault."

"No, it wasn't. You heard what the doctor said. Babies get sick. It happens all the time." She moved closer, but there seemed to be an invisible, impenetrable force around him that stopped her, just out of arm's reach.

"He was in the *hospital*."

He was beginning to scare her a little. Obviously, it was upsetting to see Zane so sick, but their son was going to be fine. The ear infection had come on so quickly. It happened, as Tabitha knew all too well.

"West, we're home now. And we're fine." She wrapped her arms around herself, but what she really wanted to do was wrap them around West.

Why did it feel like he was slipping away?

"Come to bed." She held out her hand.

He lifted his gaze to hers but didn't move a muscle. "What?"

"I don't want to sleep alone tonight. Come to bed." She wiggled her fingertips, feeling altogether too vulnerable in this moment. Earlier tonight, she'd been able to see their future so clearly. But now it kept slipping out of focus, like she was waking up from a deep, delicious dream.

Back to reality.

She could feel her heart beating in the center of her throat. Her head spun a little. If he didn't take her hand and follow her to the bedroom, she wasn't sure what she was going to do. She just needed to be held, to feel him again, skin to skin. Because then she'd know for certain that this was real—as real as the silver that had brought the miners to Chatelaine back before the search for gold had sent everything tragically tumbling down, down, down.

The moment stretched out between them until West finally rose to his feet, placed his hand in hers and let her lead him to the bedroom where he undressed her in the light of the silvery moon.

Then he made love to her, slow and sweet. Like the tenderest goodbye.

Chapter Thirteen

Chatelaine turned up on Tabitha's doorstep the following morning in full force.

She wasn't sure exactly how word of Zane's trip to the emergency room had spread around town so quickly, but first up was Betty Lawford from across the street, bearing a bouquet of roses from her garden and a batch of homemade peach jam. Then, the casseroles started rolling in, one right after another. Even Courtney stopped by with a mini-batch of her homemade ice pops. West spent the majority of the morning answering the doorbell and rearranging things in the refrigerator, while Tabitha fussed over Zane.

The baby's temperature was down—not quite back to normal, but to a mild, low-grade fever that kept him sleepy throughout much of the day. Tabitha gave him plenty of fluids, held warm compresses to his ear and made sure his blanket stayed tucked around him while he rested in his crib. Between taking care of him and the constant flow of well-wishers, she didn't have a spare second to talk to West about the night before.

She'd wanted him…*needed* him…and she had no regrets. Making love with him again had been like finally allowing herself to take a full inhale after holding her breath for a very long time. In the light of morning, everything seemed good and right and perfect. Just the way it was supposed to be.

Of course West had been upset the night before. It had been his first experience dealing with a sick child. Tabitha still remembered how panicked she'd been when the twins had come down with their first upper respiratory infection. They were so tiny and helpless. Every cough had made her go all panicky inside.

Things were fine, though. Surely West could see that. Once they had a minute or two to themselves, they'd sit down and talk about their future. They were a family now, through thick or thin. In sickness and in health.

"Tabs." West poked his head in the doorway of the nursery and rapped his knuckles gently on the door. "Look who's here. She brought lasagna."

Bea Fortune appeared beside him, waving exaggeratedly and emitting a silent squeal at the sight of Zane asleep on Tabitha's chest in the rocking chair.

"Hi, Bea. It's so great to see you." Tabitha shifted the baby in her arms and stood. Zane's tiny rosebud mouth puckered in his sleep.

"I hope I'm not disturbing you, but I wanted to help. Also…" Bea ran her hand over the small swell of her baby bump. "I might have just wanted to soak up a little bit of motherhood. This pregnancy is giving me major baby fever."

"You can come hang out with the twins anytime, and you don't need to bring anything from the Cowgirl Café with you. Although, I've never turned down lasagna in my life." Tabitha laughed, and Zane stirred.

"Oops." Bea dropped her voice to a whisper. "Can I hold him if I'm really quiet and gentle?"

"Of course you can." Tabitha transferred Zane to the other woman's waiting arms, while West grabbed a blanket to drape over the baby.

Bea's entire face lit up as soon as she got her hands on Zane. Back when Tabitha had been pregnant with the twins, she'd never once felt like she had the infamous pregnancy "glow." Grief over losing West had taken its toll, and she spent most days fighting off nausea with a sleeve of saltines while working from home in her comfiest sweatpants. Glowing, she was not.

But Bea was *luminous*. Tabitha was one of the first people she'd confided in after she'd found out she was pregnant. It had been a surprise, and it had come at a time when Bea wondered if she'd ever have children. Sometimes the most unexpected gifts really were the best ones of all. Bea and Devin's baby was going to be so loved.

"How are you feeling? Is everything going okay with the pregnancy?" Tabitha asked a little while later after Zane had gone back down for a nap in his crib.

The table was all set and the lasagna had just come out of the oven, along with a loaf of crunchy garlic bread.

"It's great, believe it or not. I feel amazing." Bea took a slice of bread from the breadbasket and then paused to take a second piece before passing the loaf to West. "I'm eating for two."

He gave Bea a crooked smile. "Indeed you are."

It was good to see him acting more like himself. They'd had a whirlwind twenty-four hours, but they'd made it. And now here they were, having dinner with family just like Tabitha had always wanted.

"How was your experience at the hospital last night? I know the emergency room isn't the same as labor and delivery, but I'd still love to hear a positive review," Bea said.

"Everyone there was great." Tabitha nodded, fork poised over her lasagna. "You've been there before, though, right?"

"Yes. Actually, I was just there recently visiting Wendell. He's been so frail lately, especially since his fall."

West frowned at his cousin. "I didn't realize Wendell was still in the hospital."

"I know. I've been meaning to talk to you about it, but you've had plenty to catch up on since you've been back," Bea said.

West sat back in his chair. "How is our granduncle doing? I can't imagine he's enjoying being in the hospital for so long."

Bea sighed. "Honestly, I'm concerned. When I was with him, he wasn't really himself. He seemed out of it."

Tabitha felt herself flinch. That didn't sound good.

"Do you think he was on some sort of medication that might have made him drowsy or confused?" she asked. It seemed like a feasible explanation.

"I don't know." Bea shook her head and absently

pushed her food around her plate with her fork. Clearly she was worried. "It was so bizarre. He started talking like he was in a daze, which I guess could have been a side effect of something they'd given him. But the things he was saying were oddly specific."

West's frown deepened. "Such as?"

"He said he'd had a child out of wedlock."

Tabitha nearly dropped her silverware. "You're right. That's *super specific* and doesn't sound at all like something he'd say just because he was drowsy."

"Oh, there's more." Bea leveled her gaze at West. Whatever was coming next must be big. "Wendell said he'd secretly acknowledged this daughter. They had a relationship, apparently, and at some point, he'd forbidden her to date a man who he didn't think was good enough for her. The boyfriend was destitute, and—here's the real kicker—"

Tabitha was riveted. So was West, judging by the expectant glint in his eyes.

Bea took a deep breath and spilled the rest. "The destitute beau apparently worked in the Fortune family silver mine here in Chatelaine."

"Oh my gosh." A million questions swirled in Tabitha's head. "What happened to him? Was he killed in the mine collapse?"

West drummed his fingers on the table. His wheels were obviously spinning just as quickly as Tabitha's were. "And what happened to the daughter?"

Bea shrugged. "I don't know. Wendell wasn't in a state to answer any questions. I just caught those bits and pieces. Do you think all of that could be true?"

"I don't see why not." West gave a mirthless laugh. "It certainly wouldn't be the first Fortune family secret."

Bea rolled her eyes. "Good point."

"It sure would be interesting to find out, though," he mused.

"I feel like we're all missing something. There are a lot of strange things going on in Chatelaine, and I can't shake the feeling that they're all somehow connected." Bea pushed her plate away and rested her forearms on the table. "Last month someone left a note on the community bulletin board that said fifty-one people had died in the mine, not fifty. The note also mentioned Gwenyth Wells, the widow of the foreman who died. No one seems to know what happened to her. And now we've got Wendell talking about a secret daughter."

"Freya has said some strange things too lately," Tabitha added, remembering their conversation outside the bookstore.

West nodded. "We ran into her the other day, and she was shaken up about the new maid at her hotel— Morgana Mills. Freya said the young woman had been following her and asking questions around town about the mine collapse."

Bea bobbed her head. "See? That's what I mean. All of this *has* to be connected, right?"

"It's certainly possible but off the top of my head, I can't see how," West said.

Tabitha waited for a beat, half expecting the old prosecutor in him to vow to get to the bottom of things.

Instead, he offered his cousin his apologies. "I'm sorry, Bea. It's been a long time since I investigated things as part of my job. I'm not really up for it anymore. For now, I'm trying to focus on being a dad."

For now. Tabitha tried not to read too much into that phrase.

"Oh, I understand. That's why I waited to even bring this up." The corner of Bea's mouth lifted. "I'm just so happy for you two. It's good seeing you together again, just like old times."

Tabitha glanced at West. Were they together in every sense of the word? She certainly thought so. They still hadn't defined things, but he had just said he needed to focus on family and that told her pretty much everything she wanted to know.

When West met her gaze, he smiled, but she could still see traces of the haunted look she'd spied in his eyes last night. Then she blinked, and it was gone.

She was worrying too much. The man she loved was still right here, and Zane was doing great. Their little family was just fine.

"You know, Bea. I have an idea." Tabitha stood and started to clear the table. "If you want to do some digging into all of this, you might want to talk to my sister, Haley."

"Oh, that's right. She's a journalist. That's a good idea," Bea replied. "Is she working on something to do with the mine collapse?"

Tabitha wished she knew. Haley was still keeping a tight lid on things. They hadn't talked about her work at all last night at the restaurant. "I'm not sure. Whatever she's working on right now is top secret. She won't even talk about it. I think it's a really big story or maybe even a book."

"I'll talk to her. Thanks for the suggestion." Bea started piling their dinner dishes in the dishwasher. "I'm going to talk to the other Fortunes too—my brothers and sisters, the other cousins and definitely Freya."

"You might try Wendell again too," West said.

"For sure." Bea nodded. "Like I said, he's still in the hospital but I heard he's doing a bit better. I need to visit him soon."

"Hopefully, you can figure out what's going on," Tabitha said.

West tossed a dish towel over his shoulder and gave them both a pointed glance. "Just remember—sometimes once you start pulling at threads, the whole mess unravels, and you end up with a much bigger problem than you anticipated."

"And sometimes you end up with a whole new understanding of your family history," Bea countered.

She simply wanted answers. Tabitha knew how West's cousin felt. Her own curiosity about her birth family was endless.

She glanced at the photo her sisters had given her for Mother's Day. It sat in its new place of honor on the mantel alongside baby pictures of the twins and a photo of West she'd clipped from the *Chatelaine Daily News* the day after the picnic in the park.

Maybe someday soon they'd add a wedding picture to the collection.

Maybe...

But for now, Tabitha tucked that thought away, like

a treasured secret. Or a sparkly diamond tucked out of sight on a golden chain.

The ring felt more at home on her finger now, though. She'd gotten used to it there. If she took it off now, she still would've felt the weight of it on her hand, like a phantom limb. Just like West's absence had taken its own shape when he'd been away. Sometimes it felt like his ghost had sucked up all the oxygen in the room, leaving her gasping for air.

Tabitha's chest ached at the memory, and she reminded herself that those days were over. She and West were standing right at the brink of a happy ending. All they had to do was hold on tight and take that final leap.

But when she looked at West while he dried the dishes, she swayed a little on her feet, as if the ground beneath her was ever so slowly slipping away.

The twins' birthday party was scheduled for just a week after Zane's hospital scare, and West woke up every single one of those days with a crushing weight pressing down on his chest.

At first, he'd thought it would get better. He'd thought that if he just tried harder to be a better dad, he could make the feeling go away. But it didn't. If anything, it grew more intense, amplified by the fact that he was now sleeping in Tabitha's bed, which made him the very worst sort of imposter.

They hadn't been intimate since the night Zane came home from the hospital. He hadn't dared go there again. That night, he'd hoped the terrible feeling inside him was only temporary. West had wanted so badly to believe that he and Tabitha belonged together that he'd ignored the warning bells going off in his head and tried to love her the way she deserved. He'd savored every breathless moment and tried to kiss away the doubt that kept pressing its way in from the outside.

However, in the cold light of morning, he realized he'd made a grave mistake. Nothing had changed. He was still his father's son, and Tabitha and the boys still deserved better. In the days since, he'd been doing his best to pretend that they were one big, happy family, as if going through the motions could make it true. And now, the night before the birthday party, in the great tradition of dads everywhere, he was up late assembling toys for the big day.

"Now *that's* a ball pit." Tabitha swished into the living room from the kitchen, where she'd been icing the homemade cake she'd baked for the party. She smelled like sweet vanilla and warm sugar, and she had a dab of buttercream frosting stuck to her forehead.

West had never seen a more beautiful woman in his entire life. His heart squeezed just looking at her.

"What do you think?" He stood up to survey his handiwork.

The pool of the ball pit was made from soft foam, secure enough to support the babies sitting in an upright position, but at the same time soft enough to prevent bumps and bruises while they played. Two hundred crush-proof, candy-colored balls filled the interior. The twins were going to have a blast.

And poor Tabitha was probably going to be chasing down stray balls until they left for college.

"I think the boys are going to love it." She surveyed the rest of the room, which had been completely taken over by wrapped packages and party decorations. "And I also think that our guests are going to be sitting on top of each other."

West took a look around. She had a point. "Maybe I should move the ball pit someplace else..."

But where?

"I have another idea." Tabitha cleared her throat, and suddenly her expression turned hesitant—bashful, almost.

And West knew without a doubt that he was once again going to let her down. He knew it before the words had even left her mouth. This was it—the moment he'd been railing against all week. He'd hoped something might change before it came. He'd hoped *he* would change.

But people rarely did.

West's parents sure hadn't. Neither had the majority of the criminals he'd put away over the course of his career.

"Tell me," he said, as if he wasn't a mere breath away from breaking her heart all over again.

It's for the best.

He should've stayed away when he'd come back to Chatelaine. The second he'd spotted those two little boys, he should've done the right thing and left Tabitha alone. Instead, he'd let himself believe in a fantasy, and he'd turned all their lives upside down in the process.

"I think we should look for a bigger house." Tabitha swallowed. "Together."

"*Together,*" West echoed, stalling for time.

He didn't want to do this, but he couldn't keep postponing the inevitable. It wasn't fair.

"Yes." She nodded, and the hopeful smile on her face wobbled, ever so slightly. "This house is just so tiny. It was already a bit small for just me and the boys, but now that we're all a family, we could really use more space. You think so too, right?"

"About the house?"

"I meant the family part, actually." Tabitha's face fell. She knew, and he hadn't even said the words yet.

But of course she knew. He'd let her down once before. Why wouldn't she expect him to do it again?

"West." She lifted her chin, eyes blazing. Her only telltale sign of vulnerability was the slight quiver of her bottom lip, which would surely be West's undoing. A tight band was beginning to form around his chest, making it impossible to breathe. "We *are* a family now, aren't we?"

Something inside West died for real right then. If it hadn't, he would've never been able to go through with it. He would've gone on pretending that he was enough, all the while knowing that he would never be the type of man that Tabitha and the twins needed.

But he couldn't do that to her. As much as it killed him to let her go, it was the right thing.

It was the *only* thing.

So he gave himself up again, just like he'd done on the riverbank. Only this time, there'd be no coming back.

* * *

Tabitha had known the end was coming.

She'd tried to tell herself that this had just been a crazy week. They'd all been shaken by Zane's trip to the emergency room. Then they'd been inundated with well-wishers while the baby was healing. Zach had only come home from Lily and Asa's house two days ago, and now she and West were neck-deep in preparations for the birthday party tomorrow.

They'd been too overwhelmed to really connect over the past few days. Too busy.

But deep down, Tabitha had known. She'd felt West slipping away from her since the night they'd taken Zane to the hospital. She just hadn't wanted to believe it.

Sometimes she wanted to squeeze her eyes closed and shut out the entire world. To pretend she'd never noticed the way West had seemed so shell-shocked as he'd answered the nurse's questions at the hospital. If she could just forget…if she could wipe her mind clean like an eraser, she wouldn't have to face the awful truth.

Because the truth was so much harder to take the second time around.

He point-blank told you he never wanted children. Why on earth would you believe that had changed?

She glared at West, all but daring him to answer the question she'd finally uttered out loud. When he refused, she asked it again for good measure—softer this time, with a rasping ache that made West wince.

"We *are* a family now, aren't we?"

Tabitha should've forced this conversation days ago, because putting off the inevitable had felt like a slow, lingering death. So much worse than a sudden gunshot wound or a fall from a riverbank. West's gradual withdrawal had been a death by a thousand paper cuts, and Tabitha had finally had enough of the pretense. If she was imagining things, he needed to tell her. Right now.

Please. She silently implored him as tears pricked the backs of her eyes. *Please tell me I'm imagining things.*

"Tabs." His gaze dropped to the floor. He couldn't even seem to look at her. "I'm sorry."

Sorry for what, exactly? For coming back to Chatelaine just when she'd been on the verge of putting the past behind her? For making her believe that he'd changed his mind about children and he wanted to get to know his sons? For making her fall for him all over again?

Tabitha truly wanted to know. But she didn't ask any of those questions because the only thing she could manage to say was the last thing he wanted to hear.

"I love you, West."

He shook his head. "No, you don't."

"But I do, and the twins love you too." She wrapped her arms around herself, as if that could somehow keep her from fully falling apart.

"Well, you shouldn't. And neither should the boys." He let out a pained sigh. "I'm not what you need, sweetheart. I'm not what the boys need. For a little while, I thought that I could be, but I'm just not."

"This is about Zane's fever, isn't it?" Of course it

was. Tabitha shook her head, incredulous. "West, I tried to tell you that babies get sick. The doctor said it too. Stop being so hard on yourself."

"It's not just about the fever. It's about everything. I wasn't here, Tabs. While you were pregnant, I was off playing cowboy."

"Because you had to fake your own death to protect me."

"Exactly. That's prime father material right there," he spat. "I never should've put you in that position to begin with."

"It wasn't your fault," she countered. Why on earth was she defending him? The man was obviously trying to break up with her.

Tabitha knew why, though. She was trying to make West see himself more clearly. It was on her to defend him because he'd never really had anyone in his corner growing up. He and his brothers had never had any sort of emotional stability. Their parents had been too wrapped up in their own drama to pay attention to their children. If Tabitha didn't defend West Fortune, who would?

"I'm just not ready for kids, and I'm not sure if I ever will be. I can't commit to the family thing right now," West said hoarsely.

It was almost word for word what he'd told her back when she'd ended their engagement. The only difference was that now there were two little boys who called him daddy.

"So what do you suggest you do instead?" Tabitha asked. It was getting harder and harder to maintain her composure when her heart felt like it was being put through a paper shredder.

"Maybe we should go back to concentrating on just being co-parents." His gaze flitted to the sofa. "I think I should go back to sleeping on the couch."

Had he completely lost his mind? This wasn't how breakups worked. It wasn't even how co-parents operated.

"And *I* think you should leave," she managed to say.

West's face crumpled for a beat before he quickly rearranged his features into a neutral expression, which made her soul shatter even more.

She slid his ring off her finger—the simple gold band and diamond solitaire that had meant so much to her while he'd been gone. Tabitha couldn't remember the last time she'd gone to sleep at night without the comforting weight of it on a chain around her neck or placed on her ring finger, just so.

Now, she placed it in the palm of his hand. Fortune family gold, returned to its rightful owner.

"I waited for you a long time, West." Forcing back the tears, she looked up at the man who'd given her the greatest gift in the world—her boys. And even though the resemblance was still unmistakable, she wasn't sure she recognized him anymore. He was just a ghost of the West Fortune she'd fallen in love with. "I can't do it anymore."

Chapter Fourteen

"We brought reinforcements." Haley held up a bag from GreatStore weighed down by what looked like a gallon of ice cream. "Cookies 'n Cream."

"Mint chocolate chip." Lily held up another bag. "And of course it's Blue Bell, because this is Texas, and our sister deserves only the best."

It had been less than half an hour since West had packed what little belongings he had and left. Tabitha wasn't even sure where he'd gone and, as she'd been reminding herself every five or ten minutes, she didn't care.

After he'd left, she'd realized she had two choices. She could either fall apart all by herself like she'd done the last time West had ridden off into the sunset without her, or she could call her sisters and let them help.

Tabitha wasn't accustomed to asking for help. She usually just powered through and handled things on her own. It was the Buckingham way, much like tennis on Saturday mornings and the country club for special holidays. But then Tabitha remembered that in Chatelaine, she wasn't a Buckingham. She was a Perry, and the Perry sisters stuck together. So she'd sent out a tearful group text to Lily and Haley, and now here they were, with enough premium Texas ice cream to choke a horse.

Sisters were the best. Tabitha wondered how she'd lasted without them for as long as she had.

"Come on in." She waved them inside. "I'll get the spoons."

They didn't bother with bowls. That seemed to go against the unwritten rules of breakups. Consolation ice cream was best eaten straight from the carton, so Tabitha and her sisters sprawled on the sofa together with their feet on the coffee table and dug right in.

"I can't believe he just up and left." Haley shoveled a comically huge spoonful of Cookies 'n Cream into her mouth.

Lily gave her a sideways glance, eyebrows raised.

"What?" Haley shrugged. "I didn't have dinner. I was working."

Lily wagged her spoon at her. "You shouldn't skip meals."

"Please," Haley said with an eye roll. "I eat ice cream for dinner on a semi-regular basis. When I'm on a deadline, I'm practically feral. Not all of us are all coupled up and living in perfect domestic bliss."

"That's right." Tabitha pointed her spoon at Lily. "Only one of us is."

"For now." Lily looked around the room, gaze flitting from the twins' wrapped birthday gifts to the ball pit still sitting in the middle of the floor where West had left it. "Look at all this. It looks pretty blissful to me. You and West really went all out. There's no way he's not showing up for the party tomorrow. Maybe tonight was just a big misunderstanding."

Tabitha's stomach churned. She hadn't considered that West might still come to the party, but surely he would. He'd rejected *her*, not the twins. Even though he felt like a failure as a dad, he still wanted to "co-parent," whatever that meant.

If he showed up tomorrow, she'd just have to put on her big girl panties and deal with it. The boys came first. West was their father, and she'd never prevent them from seeing him on their birthday.

Still, tomorrow night might require another gallon of Blue Bell.

"Unless there's a way to misinterpret the phrase 'I can't commit to the family thing right now,' it wasn't a misunderstanding," she said.

Haley pulled a face. "Ouch. He actually said that? I'm going to tell Sheriff Cooper. He needs to take back the key to the city, pronto."

"West qualified it, though. He said he couldn't commit *right now*," Lily said, ever the optimist. "He'll come back around. I know he will. He loves you, Tabitha. And he adores the boys."

The saddest part of all was that Tabitha agreed with her. She knew West loved them. She'd just always believed that love was enough.

Well, apparently it wasn't.

"I can't wait for him forever." She shook her head. "I shouldn't have to, and neither should Zach or Zane. I could never walk away from them. *Never*. If West can do it so easily, then maybe he's right. Maybe he really isn't father material."

"Something tells me he didn't find it easy. If what West really wanted was to get his old life back, he could've done that weeks ago. The sheriff all but handed it to him on a silver platter." Lily gave Tabitha a gentle shoulder bump. "He chose you instead."

"Temporarily," Tabitha reminded her.

"Was keeping things temporary West's decision, or was it yours?" Lily asked as she dipped her spoon into the carton for another bite.

"West's, obviously," she said automatically, but then she realized it wasn't quite the truth.

One day at a time. Wasn't that what she and her sisters had talked about the last time they'd had a heart-to-heart about West? Tabitha hadn't been ready to jump in with both feet. She needed time to trust West again with her heart. He'd been the one who'd seemed ready to grab life with both hands and build a new future together. As soon as he learned he was a father, he'd been all in. Tabitha had been the one who couldn't commit.

Oh, how the tables had turned.

"He's just scared, hon." Lily gave Tabitha a sad smile. "He's scared he's not enough for Zach and Zane. All those things he said tonight were just fear talking. You know that, right?"

Of course she did. She just hadn't paused long enough to put it in perspective. When West had first come back to town, she'd been scared too. She'd been terrified to her core, and instead of pushing her to commit to a whole new life, West had given her exactly what she needed.

He'd given her space. And time. He'd shown up—at home with the twins, at her parents' country club, even at playgroup. In fact, he'd been there every single day, happy to take whatever she could give him without asking or pushing for more. And the minute he'd stumbled and he'd needed her to show up for him and love him in the same unconditional way, she'd refused. She'd drawn a line in the sand, and now there was no turning back.

Oh God. What have I done?

Tabitha stared at the ball pit sitting in the center of the floor and imagined a lifetime of birthday parties where West would be nothing but a guest in her home. In his own children's hearts.

Had she rushed things? What was the time limit on waiting for someone to come back to life?

"I don't think I can eat any more of this." Tabitha placed a hand on her stomach. She felt sickeningly full and empty, all at the same time. "And can we talk about something else, please?"

Anything but West.

Haley nodded. "Sure. What do you want to talk about?"

"I know." Lily pointed her spoon at Haley. "Let's talk about *you*, and this mysterious secret project of yours."

"I like that idea." Tabitha sat up a little straighter.

Haley shook her head. "No. I can't, y'all. There's still too much to unravel."

Tabitha's mind snagged on the word *unravel*. It was

the same exact term West had used when he'd been talking to Bea about investigating all the mysterious things going around Chatelaine. Probably just a coincidence, but Bea had asked if Haley was researching the mine collapse. Maybe she was.

But if so, why all the secrecy?

"Are you working on a story about the Fortunes and the mine collapse?" Tabitha asked before she could stop herself.

Haley went quiet.

Lily gasped.

"You *are*, aren't you?" Tabitha said.

"Yes, I am." Haley took a measured inhale and finally put down her spoon. "But honestly, we should just leave it at that, okay?"

Tabitha had pushed, just like she'd pushed with West. And once again, she'd gotten an answer that didn't make her feel any better.

"Okay." She bit her lip and wondered how Bea might feel about a full-fledged investigation into the mines.

Freya, too. She'd been beside herself at the thought of Morgana asking questions. The rest of the Fortunes probably wouldn't be any happier about it either. And West? What would he think when he found out?

But as the conversation moved on to other things and Tabitha talked long into the night with her sisters, she remembered that the Fortunes weren't her concern anymore. Neither was West or his thoughts about the mine collapse.

She'd made that crystal clear when she'd given him back his ring.

* * *

West sat on the back porch of Camden's ranch house and turned Tabitha's engagement ring over in his palm.

After all this time, she'd given it back. West had been shell-shocked when she handed it to him. Even when she'd broken off their engagement two years ago, she hadn't returned the ring.

Not that he would've let her. The ring belonged to Tabitha. It would've been less painful if she'd reached into his chest, yanked out his heart and placed it in his hand instead.

"You feel like telling me what happened?" Camden asked.

They were seated side by side, facing the pasture, where horses grazed in the moonlight. The night was painfully quiet. There wasn't a cricket to be heard, just the occasional swish of the horses' tails and their hooves moving gently over the damp ground.

West loved Texas. He couldn't imagine living anyplace else. The wide-open spaces always had a way of soothing his soul. Even when he'd been on the run, gazing up at the vast blue sky had made his problems seem smaller and more manageable. He'd just *known* deep in the pit of his soul that no matter what it took he'd go home someday. Sometimes he'd choose a star—the one that shined the biggest and brightest—and he'd vow on that star that when he made it back to Chatelaine, he'd make things right with Tabitha. If fate gave him a second chance, he wouldn't waste it. Everything would be different. Perfect. Real.

Because his time away from Chatelaine hadn't felt

like real life at all. It had felt like falling into a deep, dark sleep—the kind where you couldn't wake up, no matter how hard you kicked and thrashed. It was like being able to hear real life going on around him, muffled and far away. Forever out of reach.

But those days were over. West was home now, and he'd managed to mess everything up in a matter of weeks.

"I hurt Tabitha and the boys. I told her I didn't think I could be a father." He swallowed hard. "That's what happened."

He could feel his brother's gaze on him, as hot and unforgiving as a branding iron.

"Are you going to say something?" West turned to look at him.

Camden just shook his head. "You're going to have to explain, because all anyone has heard from you since you've been back is that you wanted to get to know your sons. You promised to make Tabitha and the boys your priority. They're the entire reason you still haven't given Sheriff Cooper an answer about the job offer, right?"

"Yeah." West stared down at his hands and balled Tabitha's ring into his fist. "I gave him my answer last week. I told him no."

"Well, that just makes things as clear as mud," Camden said.

"Tabitha doesn't know. I was going to tell her, and then Zane got sick." West took a ragged inhale. "And then everything sort of spiraled from there."

"'Everything' spiraled?" Camden made annoying air quotes around the word. "Or *you* spiraled?"

West sighed. Had his younger sibling always been so adept at cutting straight to the chase? "Both, but mostly the latter."

"I don't get it, brother. I thought you said that Zane was feeling better. Aren't the boys having a big birthday party at Tabitha's house tomorrow with cake and ice cream and all that jazz?"

"Yes, and he's feeling much better. But that's not the point," West insisted.

"Then why *is* Zane getting sick such a big deal? Don't little kids get sick all the time?" Camden let out a laugh. "The three of us sure did when we were growing up. Remember when we all had the chicken pox?"

"That was—" West started.

And then they both finished the sentence in unison. "Bear's fault."

Bear's second-grade girlfriend had stayed home from school for a week with the childhood virus, and his poor lovestruck heart couldn't take her absence. He'd snuck over to her house after school and climbed through her bedroom window, like one of the heroes in the adventure stories he loved so much.

All three brothers had paid the price for that little escapade. West still had a chicken pox scar behind one of his ears.

"We survived," Camden said with a shrug.

West gave him a meaningful look. "Did we?"

He marveled at his brother's ability to put the past behind him. Camden had jumped into a relationship with both feet a while back, seemingly unfazed by their unhappy childhood. Of course that hadn't panned out, either, although West wasn't entirely sure what went wrong.

"It's my fault that Zane ended up in the emergency room," he gritted out.

"Maybe." Again, Cameron shrugged. "Maybe not."

His nonchalance was really beginning to tick West off.

"It was. If I'd known to take his temperature, the trip to the hospital could've been avoided altogether."

"Debatable. You don't have a crystal ball. No one knows what might've happened." Camden held up a hand to ward off the argument that West was ready to unleash. "But let's assume you're right. Would the outcome have been any different in the long run? Zane is *fine*. And knowing you, you now know more about baby ear infections than all the doctors at County Hospital put together."

Guilty as charged.

"I may have done some research," West admitted.

Camden rolled his eyes.

"What? A good prosecutor is always fully prepared."

"But you're not a prosecutor," Camden reminded him.

He was right. West wasn't the county prosecutor anymore, and he didn't miss it a bit.

"Old habits and all that," he muttered.

"West, you've got to let it go, man. Mom and Dad were awful parents, but that doesn't mean you're destined to follow in their footsteps. The longer you let the past mess with your head, the more you're missing out on. Zane and Zach are turning one year old tomorrow."

West gave a terse nod. "I'm aware."

He was also aware that he was probably the last person that Tabitha wanted at their birthday party. But was he really going to willingly miss it? What had happened to the man who'd once been so eager to sacrifice anything for a second chance at life? Where had *that* guy gone? West really wished he knew.

"Look, I get it. You had no idea you were a dad. The twins were the surprise of a lifetime." Camden looked at him like he wanted to give him a good, hard shake. "But everything you put yourself through for the past two years was because you love Tabitha. Why would you walk away from that now? It doesn't matter if you never wanted to be a father before. Ever since you set foot back in Chatelaine a few weeks ago, all you've done is pour your heart into those boys. You don't need to worry about learning how to be a dad. You already *are* one."

West went still and let his brother's words wash over him. But Camden wasn't finished. Just when West was about to offer a counterargument—because every trial lawyer was fully adept in the fine art of crafting a rebuttal—his sibling planted his hands on his shoulders and looked him straight in the eyes, as if doing so could sear what he said next directly onto his heart.

"And you're a *great* one." Camden's green eyes flashed, and after a tense beat, his gaze softened. "Trust me when I say this, brother. I would've given anything to have a dad like you when I was a kid."

They were just the right words at just the right time. Coming from anyone else, West wouldn't have believed them. But this was Camden. Only West knew the real meaning behind that statement. Bear would've too, if he'd been there.

West missed his other brother fiercely in that moment. It felt incomplete without all three of them.

"Thanks, man," West said quietly. He took a deep inhale and, miracle of miracles, the weight on his chest eased. Just a little bit...just enough to breathe again.

"Anytime." Camden gave his shoulder another firm pat before sitting back in his chair. "Now that we've solved that crisis, shall we fix your unemployment situation? Because I was dead serious about giving you a job. I'm neck-deep in insurance paperwork and legal documents. I want to get this camp up and running as soon as possible."

West felt the corner of his mouth tug into a half grin. Camden was getting ahead of himself, as usual. Just because West might feel slightly better about the kind of father he could be didn't mean Tabitha would be willing to give him another chance. He wouldn't blame her if she never wanted to see him again.

But he had to try. He'd never forgive himself if he didn't.

As West opened his fist and he looked at Tabitha's ring in his hand, something stirred deep inside him. He was coming back to life—and he'd do whatever it took to prove to her and his sons that this time, it was for good. It was for better, for worse. For richer, for poorer.

For all the days of his life.

"So what do you say?" Camden reached over and

flicked the brim of West's Stetson. "Do you want to leave that cowboy hat on and come work with me here at the ranch?"

West flashed his brother a smile and nodded. He was tired of standing still, letting his new life pass him by. Or waiting to feel like he deserved his good fortune. Tabitha and the twins weren't a prize he could ever earn. They were a gift—the most priceless gift of all, and all he could do was treasure them.

Gratitude burrowed deep. He needed to make some decisions, starting right now.

It was time to really start living again.

Chapter Fifteen

Zach and Zane woke up with the dawn.

In her head, Tabitha knew her sons were only a year old and couldn't possibly understand the concept of a birthday party, but in her heart, she was seriously beginning to wonder. It was as if they knew that today was special. They were like two giddy kids on Christmas morning, happily babbling to each other from their respective cribs before Tabitha had yet to open her eyes.

She cracked an eyelid and checked the time on the clock on her bedside table. Just as she suspected, the hour was obscenely early. It might not have felt quite so obscene if she hadn't stayed up so late gabbing with Lily and Haley the night before.

Had they really eaten two full gallons of ice cream? Yes. Yes, they had. And Tabitha refused to feel a single drop of remorse about it. *Self-care.* Wasn't that what the internet called it? Everyone knew that there were five steps to surviving a breakup and the first step involved ice cream.

Or maybe she was getting things confused with the five stages of grief. Tabitha certainly knew a thing or two about that as well. She'd been ping-ponging between all fives stages for the better part of two years. Just when she thought she'd reached the fifth and final stage—*acceptance*—she plunged right back down to the start again. It was like being permanently strapped inside the world's most depressing roller-coaster ride.

Would it ever end?

Not today, it won't. With a resigned sigh, she climbed out of bed, slipped into her favorite fuzzy pink bathrobe and headed toward the nursery. Maybe she should've taken Lily and Haley up on their offer to stay the night. Just the thought of getting through the day seemed nothing short of exhausting. The party was set to start in a few short hours, and she needed to get the boys up, fed and ready before the guests arrived, all while navigating her way back to stage number one: *denial*.

Had last night really happened? Tabitha tried to tell herself it had only been a bad dream, but no amount of denial could hide the fact that West was gone. Her head hadn't been resting on his broad shoulder when she'd opened her eyes. His long legs weren't stretched out on her sofa. And to make matters worse, the ball pit he'd been so proud of was still sitting in the middle of the living room, mocking her in all of its cheery, candy-hued glory.

She'd really done it. She'd given him his ring back and told him to leave.

He'd hurt her, and this time, the wound had cut her to the quick. There was a limit to how many times a heart could break and then somehow manage to stitch itself back together. As far as Tabitha could tell, that limit was three times.

Third time's the charm. She pressed the heel of her hand against the raw ache in her chest as she paused near the nursery door. *Once, when we called off the engagement. Twice, when West "died." And again, last night, when all my hopes and dreams perished for good...*

Yes, the number was definitely three. Although, so far, the healing part hadn't even started. She still had to get through all five lovely stages first, and so far, her heart had planted its flag firmly in *denial* and refused to move.

If only he'd fight for me this time. Fight for us...

Tabitha gave her head a good, hard shake. She'd given West his ring back. She couldn't have given him a clearer signal if she'd tried. They were over. Period. He had probably already moved into the county prosecutor's office with a sleeping bag by now. And Sheriff Cooper was no doubt planning another over-the-top party.

Fine. Tabitha had her own party to worry about today, and the twins would never have another first birthday. She needed to pull herself together, paste on a smile and do what good mothers had been doing since the dawn of time: put her children first. She could fall apart later after the candles had been blown out and the floor was littered with crumpled wrapping paper.

"Mama." Zach peered at her over the rails of his crib. "Mama, mama, mama."

Zane joined in, pulling himself up to standing and calling out to her in a singsong voice. "Mamamamama."

"Good morning, my sweeties," she said in a gentle whisper. "Happy birthday."

And against all odds, she smiled. The three of them were going to be okay. They really were. They'd made their way through this storm before, and they could do it again. So long as Tabitha had her boys, she'd be all right.

She got the twins changed and decided to feed them breakfast in their pajamas so their new Western-themed birthday outfits wouldn't get messy before the party. It had been a while since she'd handled the morning routine completely on her own. Like most cowboys, West was an early riser. He'd thrived with the boys in the early morning hours when he'd been living there.

But Tabitha fell back into her single-mom routine with ease—on the outside, anyway. *Denial, denial, denial.*

She'd just put the boys in their matching highchairs and begun gathering the ingredients for pancakes when Zach and Zane started babbling again. She smiled to herself. She needed this today. Nothing warmed her heart quite like the sound of her babies saying *mama*.

"Dada?" Zane said.

Tabitha froze. She'd been completely unprepared for the twins to ask for West. She'd thought they could go right back to the way they'd been before—back to a time when the boys had never known their father at all.

How could she have been so foolishly naive?

"Honey, Daddy's not here right now," she said, voice trembling.

"Dada," Zane said again, kicking his legs in his highchair.

Zach immediately started parroting his brother. "Dada."

"I'm sorry, boys, but Daddy isn't here," Tabitha whispered. She could barely get the words out.

He's not here because I told him I wouldn't wait for him anymore. I told him to leave, even though that's the very last thing I wanted.

Tabitha's throat closed up tight. She couldn't do this. She couldn't pretend that West's presence in their lives, even for a short time, had never made a difference. Zach and Zane would never be the same after knowing their father, and that was a good thing. They deserved all the love in the world—more love than Tabitha could give them all on her own. Whatever West could offer his sons, she'd take it.

Seeing him again would hurt. There was no doubt about that, but the boys needed him. They *loved* him, and whether West realized it or not yet, he loved them, too.

"Dada," Zane said again.

Tabitha took a deep breath and turned toward her son, willing herself not to cry. "Daddy's not here right now," she repeated, "but we'll see him again soon. I'm going to make sure he knows that you want him to come to your birthday party."

Zane's little forehead scrunched and then his gaze shifted, so he was looking over her shoulder. "Dada." He pointed toward the window overlooking the front porch.

A shiver coursed through Tabitha as she turned around. *No*, she told herself. *It can't be.* West had already given her the surprise of her life when he'd been waiting for her on the front steps after playgroup a few weeks ago. He wasn't going to just keep turning up again until she decided to give him another chance.

He didn't *want* another chance.

But there he was, sitting on the top step, right where he'd been before. Just like last time, his black Stetson was pulled down low over his eyes.

Tabitha's heart nearly leapt straight out of her chest.

"Dada," Zane said in his singsong voice.

"That's right, baby. Daddy's home." Tabitha's hands trembled as she lifted him from the highchair and then did the same for Zach.

She put the boys on the floor and led them by their little hands to the front door. When she opened it and stepped outside, West didn't budge. The poor guy was sound asleep, sitting straight up and leaning against the porch railing. A massive bouquet of yellow roses sat beside him, tied with a white satin ribbon.

Tabitha could hardly believe it. He was back, and he'd *slept* there.

He must've shown up sometime after Lily and Haley had gone home the night before. All the while she'd been missing him, he'd been right there, keeping the promise he'd made her when he'd first come home.

I'm not going anywhere. You have my word.

How could Tabitha have forgotten that West Fortune's word was as good as gold?

"Dada!" Zane cried.

West's eyes drifted open. He squinted against the morning sun, and then blinked as his gaze homed in on Tabitha and the boys.

"Good morning, cowboy." She nodded toward the

house across the street, where Betty Lawford's profile was clearly visible peeking out from behind a lace curtain in her front window. "You're really determined to keep the neighbors around here talking, aren't you?"

West looked up at her with eyes full of questions, and Tabitha's unspoken answer to every single one of them was an unqualified yes. She nodded, and when he stood to gather her in his arms, he held onto her so tight that she thought he'd never let go.

"I'm so sorry," he whispered into her hair. "Of course we're a family. Always have been, always will be."

"Always," she said through tears.

"I love you, sweetheart. Don't cry. Please don't. Today's a day to celebrate." He handed her the roses and then bent to scoop a twin into each of his arms. "Happy birthday, boys."

Zane tipped his head back and laughed.

"Buday," Zach said.

Tabitha gasped. "Did he just say birthday?"

Zach squealed, utterly pleased with himself. "Buday."

"That's right, son. It's your birthday." West beamed at him. "But why don't we take this little pre-party inside? Betty has probably had enough excitement for one day."

West didn't want to leave anything unsaid.

He'd made that mistake before, and he had no intention of doing it again. Life was precious. Everything could change in a blink of an eye. He needed Tabitha to know he was all in this time. So later, once the party was in full swing and the boys were busy playing in their ball pit for an audience of all their loved ones, West slipped his hand in Tabitha's and tugged her into the only quiet corner of the house.

"Hi, there," he said once they were alone in Tabitha's bedroom.

She grinned up at him. "Hi, yourself. Is everything okay?"

"Everything is better than okay. Everything's perfect." He held up a finger. "With just one exception."

Her brow furrowed, and before she could ask him to elaborate, he dropped to one knee.

"West!" Tabitha gasped softly. "You really don't need to do this…"

"On the contrary. It's very necessary." He took her ring from his pocket and slid it back onto her finger where it belonged. "I know we've already said we're a family, but I want us to make things official. I want to marry you, Tabs—preferably as soon as possible. But if you want a big, fancy wedding, I'll wait."

"You mean at my parents' country club?" She winked at him.

West pretended to consider the suggestion. Not that she was at all serious. "I don't know. I'm just a small-town lawyer with a part-time private practice. I don't think I rank high enough for a wedding at someplace that fancy."

Tabitha's eyes went wide. "You're…*what*? You're not going back to work as the county prosecutor?"

He shook his head and said simply, "Nope."

"Nope? Just like that?" A burst of laughter escaped her, and she clamped her hand over her mouth.

"Just like that. I actually turned the job down last week and hadn't found the right time to tell you. Camden has asked me to help him with some legal matters at the ranch. I'm going to be working with him for a while, and I thought maybe I'd open a part-time practice in town. Folks around here need legal help sometimes, and I might be the right man for the job. It probably won't be enough work to keep me busy full-time, so you might have to get used to having me around the house." He flashed her a grin. "Correct me if I'm wrong, but you seem okay with that decision."

"I'm over the moon. This is the best news I've heard all day." She glanced down at her ring and wiggled her finger. "Correction—second best."

"So the answer is yes? You'll marry me?"

"I love you. Try and stop me, cowboy." She gave his hand a tug. "Now stand up and kiss me."

"So bossy," West said as he rose to his feet. Then he dipped his head and brushed a featherlight kiss to her lips, but it was just a prelude.

"One last thing," he murmured against her warm, sweet mouth.

Nothing left unsaid.

"It had better be important," she whispered as she wound her arms around his neck.

"This house. You're right…it's far too small. I vote we start looking for something bigger right away." He pulled back, just far enough so he could meet her gaze. "And since we'll be moving, we should probably find someplace big enough for a third baby. Zane and Zach would make great big brothers to a new little one, don't you think?"

Tabitha beamed at him. When she smiled like that, with her whole, beautiful face, West felt warm all over. "Are you serious right now, West Fortune?"

"I've never been more serious about anything in my life." Life was for living, and West had wasted enough time. Never again. "I'm all in, beautiful."

"So am I. Let's do it. Let's have another baby," Tabitha whispered, as if they were sharing their own special secret.

They'd share their good fortune with their friends and family soon enough, but for now, these promises were theirs and theirs alone. West and Tabitha had finally found their new beginning, and it started with a happy-ever-after.

Sealed with a kiss.

* * * * *

Haley Perry arriving in Chatelaine hot on a scoop, dredging up the disaster at the Fortune Silver Mine, is Camden Fortune's nightmare come true. But Haley's got a way of convincing Camden to join forces to discover the truth.

Watch her investigation—and their mutual attraction!—sizzle in

Worth a Fortune
By Nancy Robards Thompson,

coming June 2024!

And until then, catch up with the whole Chatelaine Fortunes clan:

Fortune's Baby Claim
By Michelle Major

Fortune in Name Only
By Tara Taylor Quinn

Expecting a Fortune
By Nina Crespo

Available now!